CLAIMED BY CRAYSON

SHERELLE GREEN

To my cousin Shenelle for planting the seed and helping me bring Jordyn's character to life and my girl Keema for all the inspiration!

To my Book Euphoria queens, ya'll are the real deal and I don't know what I would do without you ladies! Special shout out to Anita, Angie, Leslie, Nicole and Sheryl for encouraging me to 'do me' and keep my storyline authentic to the vision I had. Every author needs friend's to convince them to jump off the cliff without hesitation and reassurance that they will be right there with them to offer support.

To Matysha, otherwise known as #HashtagQueen! Thank you for always supporting me and my work, especially the Madden brothers!

To my S-Squad for supporting me this year as I branched out into a different series! I appreciate each of you ladies!

#CLAIMEDBYCRAYSON

If there were ever a man who prided himself on always being up front with women, it's tatted bad boy, Crayson Madden, in the flesh. His world may revolve around sex and cigars, but there's a lot more to this cigar lounge owner than what meets the eye. Too bad Jordyn Jameson spends more time arguing with him, than seeing beyond his asshole-ish ways. Now, they are forced together whether she likes it or not and the more Crayson pushes her buttons, the more he likes what he sees behind the confident siren.

Dessert bar owner, Jordyn Jameson, would rather poke her eyes out than spend time with the certified playboy. Unfortunately, this creator of tasty treats doesn't have a choice in the matter. Crayson has recipe for disaster written across his sexy forehead and the one thing she's learned from her past, is that men like Crayson were good for one thing and one thing only. She knows he wants her in his bed, and although she may be tempted, she's not giving in. Besides, she has bigger things on her mind. Jordyn has been harboring a big secret and needs help fast. The irony of it all? The last man she'd ever sleep with may be the only one to help ensure that her secret stays that way.

ONE

Crayson

SOME WOULD CALL ME AN UNAPOLOGETIC ASSHOLE. Others would call me a tatted bad boy with no filter. What I say is what I mean, even if it hurts your feelings or makes me sound like an idiot sometimes.

I've been called a lot of things in my lifetime, but rarely am I described as charming, unless the word is followed by son-of-a-bitch.

The first time a woman called me a charming son-of-a-bitch, I was whispering dirty nothings into her ear while her legs were spread high as I fucked her until her husband got home. Yeah, I said it. She was a married woman, and even though it wasn't my proudest moment, in my defense, I hadn't known she was married at the time.

I was sixteen back then and I'd met her at a bar. Within moments of us meeting, she'd been pushing her chest into my face quicker than I could down the glass of Hennessy I'd gotten thanks to my fake ID. She hadn't been wearing a ring, and by the time we'd reached her place, our clothes were flying off so fast, I didn't think to stop and look for some fucking family photos.

Back then, I'd known damn well I shouldn't have been three hours away from home on some dumb shit with the lowlifes I used to kick it with. My dick had been doing all of the talking when I'd met ... Shit. I don't even remember her name anymore. Her name didn't matter anyway. As I was hightailing my black ass out of her window when her husband got home, I surprisingly hadn't been too occupied to hear her try and explain that she'd been lonely for years in a loveless marriage. As heartless as it sounds, I hadn't given a shit at the time. I was too busy trying not to catch a case with her husband who saw me the moment I'd gotten to the window.

Bottom line, ever since I was sixteen, I'd come to terms with the man I was meant to be. The asshole I was supposed to be. The condescending dude who did as he damn well pleased regardless of the consequences. I didn't have to listen to anyone. I controlled my actions. No one told me what to do because I wouldn't change for nobody. *Refused* to change for anybody.

"Crayson, hurry the hell up. I want to get to the resort before sunset."

"Damn, I'm coming." Except when it came to my brothers apparently. When it came to my brothers, it didn't matter that in weight and muscle, I was bigger than all of them. Unlike some people who took one look at my tattoos and size and thought twice about fucking with me, my brothers didn't care. They'd always tease me or tell me what to do, and in some ways, I appreciated them for that. It took me down a notch and kept me humble.

I was the type of mutha fucka who you couldn't let get away with shit. If you gave me an inch, I'd take a foot. If you extended me an olive branch, odds were I'd be uprooting the whole damn tree. So yeah, I appreciated my brothers for calling me on my shit, but I'd never tell them that.

"Not too much longer," one of my brothers yelled.

Fuck, I'm over this shit. I glanced up from my chest to acknowledge my brother, Malik, since my head was buried deep into my North Face coat. "Damn B, if I wanted to freeze my balls off, I could have stayed my ass in New York." Did I sound like the usual asshole that I was? Sure. Was I going to change if I hadn't in thirty-three years? Probably not. Did I give a damn? Not really.

I shivered as I followed my brothers down the side of the snowy mountain we'd just hiked from. Colorado in late December wasn't exactly my idea of a vacation, but Malik loved snow and cold shit, so I should have known he would pick someplace like Colorado since it was his time to choose our bi-annual brothers' trip.

Growing up with five brothers had been a lot of fun, but now that folks were grown, getting married, having kids, and starting businesses and shit, we had to make sure we carved out some time for each other. When Micah got married over four years ago, we decided to try and do at least two guy-only trips together. So far, we'd kept to our word. My brother, Carter, was the only one who hadn't made a trip yet, but we hadn't seen him years.

Originally, I'd thought this was gonna be a relaxing snowboarding trip in which we hit the mountain for a little bit, then spent the remainder of the week at the resort or exploring the city. Little had I known, Malik had planned for us to do a bunch of bonding activities like hiking on a cold ass mountain, ice skating, dog-sledding, and ice fishing.

Okay, so maybe the dog-sledding and ice skating was kinda cool, but ice fishing? I didn't catch a damn thing, and I was pretty sure I'd lost all feeling in one of my big toes a couple days ago from my foot slipping into the icy water.

"Why the hell is he always so dramatic?" my brother, Malakai, asked. I didn't respond since I knew the question wasn't for me. Any time they talked about me like I wasn't there, they didn't expect me to respond. Or they expected me to respond, but planned on ignoring whatever I had to say.

"Like Mama always says, Crayson was born overly-dramatic." Caden shook his head. "I knew we should have left him in New York. He's gonna complain the whole rest of the trip."

Caden, Carter, and I were identical triplets, but I didn't have much in common with my brothers. Caden and Carter had always been close growing up, and a part of me thought Caden and I would get closer once Carter joined the military, but we weren't. At least, not anymore than usual. Sure, I loved them, but sometimes I wished they understood me more.

Hell, I wished most of my family understood me more. Everyone in my family had a role to play, and as badly as I wanted my role to be different sometimes, I'd embraced it by now. To those who knew the Madden brothers best, they were familiar with our roles. Investigator Malik was the intelligent one. Security firm owner Micah was the protector. Painter and sculptor Malakai was the artist. Rodeo cowboy Caden was the southern gentleman. MIA Carter was the distinguished military man. And me ... I was the one my family thought would be a fuck-up, but had turned out pretty decent. I owned a couple cigar lounges in New York — soon to be three —, so I'd done well for myself.

Unfortunately, I was still labeled as that "other" Madden brother. The one with no filter. City boy Crayson, otherwise known as asshole extraordinaire.

"Shit," Micah cursed as his boots sunk deeper into the snow. "I sort of agree with Crayson. This is the last time we let Malik choose the location."

Malik turned back to glare at the group. "Bruh, you all agreed to come months ago, so don't blame me since you can't handle a little cold. If Malakai is good, ya'll have to stop complaining."

"I'm good," Malakai co-signed. Our bro trip had been planned a while ago, but now, it gave us a chance for us to celebrate Malakai's recent engagement. Although I was proud of my big brother, I was cold as hell and whenever I was cold, I couldn't think straight.

I slipped in the snow as we continued downhill and caught myself before I fell too hard. "Once upon a time, there were five brothers who climbed a mountain never to be seen again."

"Shut it," Malik said. "We're almost there."

"Thank God." My sentiment was followed by similar ones from Caden and Micah even though they'd given me a hard time earlier. The view at the top had been beautiful, just like the concierge at the resort had stated, but hypothermia was a real thing and I needed to get indoors ASAP.

"Since we're close to the resort, there's something I need to tell you fellas."

We all directed our attention to Malakai as much as we could without slowing down as we neared the end of the snowy hike.

Malakai glanced forward at Malik before turning to look at the rest of us. "Malik already knows this, but I was talking to Avery a couple weeks ago about the trip and she mentioned that her and her friends had planned on coming to Colorado on a ski trip next month. So I may or may not have suggested she come this weekend instead."

"You shitting me," I yelled. "You see Avery every damn day and you decided to invite her on our guys' trip, too?"

Sighing, Caden turned toward Malakai. "Bro, you know I don't mind that you invited her and her friends to crash our trip. Hell, Micah and Malik did that shit the first couple years we started taking these trips. But you know Crayson is sensitive about his brotherly time, so you could have given the rest of us a heads-up so we could prepare for his bitching."

My teeth chattered as I claimed, "I don't bitch. I complain. There's a distinct difference." I was sure they all shared a look, but I was too busy trying not to bust my shit again as I shivered. I'd fallen enough on this trip. "All I'm saying is that I think a few of you are forgetting the meaning of a guy-only trip. I love the ladies just like the next mutha fucka, but these trips—even in this cold ass weather—should be a time for us to re-connect as brothers. Y'all can see your wives and fiancée when you get home."

"I hear you." Malakai cleared his throat as they approached the side entrance of the resort. "Would your opinion change, though, if I told you that Avery managed to talk a certain bar owner into letting her manager handle business this weekend so she could take this trip?"

My eyebrows perked up. "Word? Jordyn agreed to come to Colorado?"

Malakai nodded his head. "Yep."

Malik glanced back at him. "Still feel the same way about this being a guys-only trip."

I was about to say, "Hell yeah," but a quick glance

through the grand window of the resort that had a clear view of the registration desk had me changing my tune.

There she was. The sexiest woman in New York. A woman so fly, I dared any man in New York—better yet, the world—to take one glance at that smooth brown face, thick, hourglass thighs, and apple bottom ass and not be ready to jack off just at the sight of her.

Jordyn Jameson wasn't your average woman and I'd known that from the minute I'd first laid eyes on her. I've always appreciated the beauty of a woman, and despite my asshole-ish ways, even if a woman didn't recognize her own beauty and worth ... I did. Most people didn't think I had substance because instead of saying something sweet and charming to or about a woman, I tended to say things more like, "I wonder if my dick will get hard every time I see her."

"You're so poetic." Malakai laughed and shook his head. "I hope that's not the pick-up line you use on her, because Jordyn isn't one of these water-head women you mess with. She has class."

I licked my lips as Jordyn laughed at something Malakai's fiancée, Avery, had said. "She sure does have class." My eyes looked her up and down. "And sass. And ass. And—"

"I think we get the picture," Malik said.

Micah shrugged. "Should've let him finish. I was curious how many other rhyming words he had in him to describe her."

I watched her lean over the registration desk, giving me a beautiful view of her backside. "Plenty." I never lacked words to describe Jordyn.

"Let's go inside before Crayson starts drooling in the snow," Malakai suggested. "Plus, I need to see my beautiful fiancée."

I followed my brothers inside, opting to be last because I knew the moment Jordyn saw me and I opened my mouth, she was either going to roll her eyes at me or curse me out. I'd take either since riling her up was one of my favorite pastimes.

"I didn't know this resort let such beautiful women stay here." Malakai snuck up on Avery and pulled her to him.

Avery slapped Malakai on the shoulder. "You're so corny." She melted into him. "And I love you for it."

While my other brothers exchanged pleasantries with Serenity and Tyler, my eyes were zoned in on Jordyn who was already giving me the death stare. I took a couple steps toward her, ignoring the warning in her eyes.

"Hey, JayJay," I teased since I knew she hated when I called her that nickname. Sure, her friends could call her that. But me? She wasn't having it.

She crossed her arms over her chest, her voice firm when she whispered, "Don't call me that, CrayCray. You don't want these problems."

I threw my head back in a laugh. Her nickname for me didn't bother me nearly as much as she wished it did. Little did she know, I smiled on the inside at the fact that she even gave me a nickname. It meant she cared. "I want any problem you're willing to give me. Just say the word and we can stop playing this cat and mouse game. Everybody already knows you want me."

She rolled her eyes. "Ugh, you're annoying as hell. Had I known you'd be in Colorado, I would have stayed in New York."

Avery jumped into the conversation. "I needed you here." She glanced from Jordyn to me, before looking at Malakai. "We both needed you here."

I raised an eyebrow. "What for?"

Avery shuffled from one foot to the other. "To talk to you about something." She glanced to the rest of the group. "Actually, we wanted to talk to everyone about something."

Malakai laughed and scratched the back of his neck the way he often did when something wasn't going the way he'd originally planned.

"What my fiancée is trying to say, is that dinner is on us tonight because we have something important to ask each of you."

Several people asked why they couldn't tell us now, but Tyler's voice was the one that stood out above the crowd. "Why all of the secrets? We already know you're asking us to be in your wedding. Quit being all 007 with us."

Avery sighed. "We wanted it to be a surprise."

"Girl, please," Tyler waved a hand. "The people you both trust most are standing in this resort lobby, so it's obvious you want us all in your wedding."

Malakai clasped his hands together. "Well, since the cat is out of the bag, what do you say, gang? Would you do Avery and I the honor of being in our wedding party?"

Tyler was the first to respond. "Hell yeah. You know I'm down."

"Glad to hear it," Avery said with a smile. "So you're good with being my HBIC?"

Tyler placed his hand over his chest. "Why, Miss Avery, are you asking me to be the head bitch in charge? Because you already know I get shit done."

"Something like that," she replied with a laugh. "Serenity, my sister, and a close friend of mine from back home are going to be bridesmaids. But, Ty, I want you to be the head *bridesmaid* in charge."

Tyler shrugged. "Bridesmaid. Bitch. Same thing."

Avery turned to Jordyn. "And, Jordyn, although I

planned on asking you this in a really cute way ... could you be my maid of honor?"

Jordyn's hands flew to her mouth. "Chick, are you serious? You want mwah as your maid of honor?"

"Of course I do," Avery smiled. "You've had my back since I moved to New York, and we've grown closer than I ever could have imagined. I would love if you could do me the honor of being by my side on the most important day of my life."

Jordyn teared up, and the moment caught me off guard because I'd never seen Jordyn get emotional over anything. Granted, most the time we spent together, she was chewing my head off about something, but this was a different look for her. The woman wasn't even trying to give me the time of day, but my head was already too far up her ass to even acknowledge others in the room whenever she was in the same vicinity. *And what an ass it was.*

The fact that Jordyn sometimes threw me off of my game was further proven when Malakai shook me out of my Jordyn-daze to ask, "Did you hear me, bro?"

I slightly shook my head. "What did you say?"

He gave my brothers a knowing look before turning his attention back to me. "You may be a pain in my ass sometimes, but I want to know if you could be my best man?"

"Ya boy?" I joked, placing my hand over my heart. "All these cats and you're choosing me to be your best man?"

"You a fool," Micah said.

"Yes, my dude." Malakai slapped me on the shoulder. "I would love for you to be my best man."

"Let's do this shit then." I was sure I was sporting a Chuck E Cheese grin as I pulled by brother in for a hug, but I didn't care. When it came to love, Malakai hadn't had an easy journey, so I was proud to walk by his side on the most important day of his life.

"On that note," Avery began, clasping her hands together, "maybe we should all get cleaned up and head to dinner?"

Everybody nodded their heads or voiced their agreements, but my eyes were focused solely on Jordyn. I told myself to chill on the teasing, however I couldn't help but say, "I guess we'll be spending even more time together."

She rolled her eyes in typical Jordyn style before she followed the others to the escalators.

It was cool that she was trying to ignore me. Someone should have told her that watching her walk away was one of my favorite pastimes.

TWO

Crayson

MAN, WHERE THE HELL DID SHE RUN OFF TO? DINNER had been over for a half hour and everyone was almost finished with dessert. Before folks had even finished their food, Jordyn had excused herself to go to the bathroom and I hadn't seen her since.

"Where's your girl?" I whispered to Serenity so that I wouldn't interrupt Avery's official thank you speech for all of us agreeing to be in her wedding.

"Where do you think?" she whispered back. "You ran her off."

I shrugged. "I didn't even do shit. All I did was eat my food."

The look she gave me was of pure disbelief. "You're always on some sneaky shit when it comes to her. So although I don't know what you did, I know you did something to run her off."

It was true. Typically, I was doing something that pissed Jordyn off. But tonight, I had simply been enjoying her company. "Did she go to her room?"

Serenity shook her head. "No."

She answered too fast. "What room is she in?"

"Nope." She shook her head. "My lips are sealed."

"Come on, Serenity. I already know you both are rooming together."

"Boy, did you not hear me?" she murmured. "I'm not telling you. I care too much about my life, and Jordyn will kill me if I tell you our room number." She upturned her nose before she turned back to listen to Avery. Serenity and I went way back, so I knew that look. She wasn't going to give up the room number, which meant I had to get creative. Especially since there were four floors in the lodge.

I glanced at Caden who I knew had been listening to my conversation with Serenity. Growing up, my brothers and I used to tease Caden by saying he should wear bells around his neck because you never knew when he entered a room. He was quiet and tended to observe the situation before speaking. Him and Carter were alike in that way.

When I caught Caden's eye, I nodded my head in Serenity's direction to get some assistance. I didn't have to spell out the situation. He knew. He waited a few minutes before baiting her.

"Serenity," he whispered. "Did you hear about that bed bug scare they had here last week?"

Serenity sat straighter in her seat. "Bed bugs? You can't be serious." Anyone who knew Serenity knew that there wasn't anything she hated more than bed bugs. When she'd initially moved to New York, she'd purchased most of her furniture from a small store she'd seen an ad for on social media. After about a week of waking up to bites all over her body, she got rid of her bed and started sleeping on her couch, only to wake up to even more bites. She'd had her furniture for three weeks before she found out everything was infested with bed bugs, so she had to have the entire place fumigated. She'd been sensitive about the situation ever since.

"Yeah, but the good news is, they only had to evacuate a few rooms on one floor," Caden said, nodding his head.

Her eyebrows lifted as she muttered, "Rooms. Did you just say rooms? What floor did this happen on?"

Caden twisted his eyes to the ceiling as if he were thinking hard about her question. "I can't remember. I think maybe it was the fourth floor."

"Thank God." She placed her hand over her heart.

My brother glanced to me before looking back to Serenity. "I meant the third floor."

"What!" she yelped. "The third floor? I'm on the third floor! I can't handle another bed bug situation. Please tell me it isn't room 305."

Caden looked to me and smiled. *Bingo.* The look didn't go unnoticed by Serenity as it dawned on her that she'd been played by Caden.

Serenity playfully hit myself and Caden on our shoulders before saying, "I can't stand y'all."

I laughed before telling them what they already knew was coming. "If anyone asks, tell them I went to the bathroom."

I slipped away from the table just as Malakai started speaking. He made some joke about me leaving, but I didn't care. I'd just ask Malik for the cliff notes version later.

When I exited the elevator and headed to Jordyn's room, I had an extra pep in my step. Although she may slam the door on my face the moment she noticed it was me, I didn't care. As lame as it sounded, I just wanted to see her.

I stepped up to room 305 and knocked. To my surprise, she opened the door right away. I was about to make a snarky remark about her being happy to see me, but the sight of her in leggings and a plain white tee caught me off guard. It wasn't until this moment that I recalled I'd never seen her in casual clothes before. Maybe jeans and a nice top, but never anything comfy-casual.

Jordyn was one of those women who looked good in anything. Her edgy, short hairstyle was sexy on her diamond head shape, the curly cut making me want to run my fingers through it. A few times over the past few months, I'd noticed my hand raising at its own accord to run my fingers through her curls. Then luckily, common sense kicked in and I remembered black women would cut you if you touched their hair without permission.

She must have been irritated that I hadn't yet told her my reason for stopping by her room, because her voice was dripping with annoyance when she asked, "What do I owe the displeasure of this visit?"

I smirked. "Can I come in?"

"Not until I know why you're here."

"I can tell you when I come in."

She crossed her arms over her chest. "Serenity texted me saying that you and Caden tricked her into telling you our room number, so you might as well just tell me whatever it is that you thought you would accomplish by coming up here."

I peeked over her shoulder into her hotel room and spotted a bottle of wine. "I have a couple ideas about the engagement party we have to plan for Avery and Malakai. Some of the details can't wait until we get back to New

York, so I was hoping we could have a nightcap and discuss it."

Her facial features softened as she studied my eyes, obviously trying to see if I was telling the truth. The excuse I'd given her was complete bullshit, but I was damn proud for thinking of something that sounded like a legit reason I'd need to see her.

Apparently, she believed me because a few seconds later she stepped out of the doorway and motioned for me to come in. The first thing I was hit with when I walked into the room was a sensual scent that came from whatever lotion or perfume she was wearing. I'd smelled it before, but at a bar or event, it usually mixed with other scents. This time, the smell slapped me across the face, causing me to subconsciously rub my jaw as if I'd really been hit.

She poured herself a glass of red wine before taking a seat opposite of the chair I'd just sat down in.

"Okay, shoot," she said before taking a sip.

I looked at her incredulously. "What about my wine?"

"You don't get wine until I decide if you're really in my hotel room to discuss plans for Avery and Malakai or something else."

Something else. It's always something else. "Damn, it's like that?"

"Hell yeah."

In that case, you better think of something. "Well, I'm not sure if you heard, but I'm opening up a new cigar lounge and the grand opening will be in a few months. I was thinking it would be nice to have the engagement party at my new location before it opens to the public."

She shrugged. "I'm fine with that."

"Great. When do you think you can come by and see the location so we can get to planning?"

She scrunched her forehead in thought. "Before we get into that, why are we the ones planning the engagement party? Don't the parents of the bride and groom usually plan that, and the maid of honor and best man plan the bachelor and bachelorette parties?"

Yes, but I need an excuse to see you more. I'd be the first to admit that I wasn't the relationship type. I liked my freedom too damn much to be tied down to one woman. But I wasn't the type of man to screw over the women I slept with either. Any woman who laid in my bed knew damn well that I was the type to fuck 'em and leave 'em, and I was man enough to admit that. If they wanted to cuddle and shit, they had the wrong guy.

Jordyn had called my card the first night we met, and ever since, she'd been ignoring my advances. In my opinion, and the opinion of our friends, she had every right to call me on my bullshit, but that didn't stop me from wanting to fuck her. My dick had been craving to be inside of Jordyn, and it was in those rare moments when she stopped the façade and let her lust shine through those sexy brown eyes that kept me shooting my shot. The day I felt like she was truly uninterested would be the day I stopped trying to sleep with her.

"My parents live in Arkansas and Avery's live in Tennessee, so I'm sure both sets of parents plan on throwing a party for them in their hometowns, but you and I need to cover New York. I'd already mentioned it to Malakai tonight and he seemed interested in having an engagement party in New York."

Once again, I was spitting a load a shit, but it sounded like the truth. I knew I'd had her convinced when she nodded her head and told me, "Sounds good. If you give me the address, I'll see how far it is from my bar so I can stop by at a decent time."

I was sure the smile that filled my face looked as sneaky as I felt when she asked, "What aren't you telling me?"

Leaning back in my chair, I crossed my hands in front of me. I should've told her the reason I was so amused right away, but I liked to fuck with her. A squirmy Jordyn was a bothered Jordyn, and a bothered Jordyn was a sexy Jordyn.

A two-minute stare down later, she gave me an ultimatum. "You have two seconds to tell me what you're holding back from telling me, or this nightcap is over."

I didn't put it past Jordyn to kick me out. She'd kicked me out of her bar a few times for no reason other than the fact that I was annoying her. She placed her wine glass on the table and sat up straighter in her chair.

"Spit it out, Madden."

I smiled. *Here goes nothing.* "I wanted to tell you a month ago, but I was afraid that you'd never speak to me again. I didn't even tell Malakai because I couldn't risk him telling Avery who I was sure would tell you."

Her eyes widened, the annoyed expression on her face still in place. "Spit. It. Out."

"Do you remember Blackberry Restaurant?" I asked. "That place I used to love to grab breakfast at?"

She squinted her eyes. "You mean the Blackberry Restaurant that's right next door to my bar?"

"Was next door," I said. "It closed a couple months ago, but I know you already knew that because we were all talking about it at the bar one day. I'm sure you noticed the for sale sign was gone."

Dropping her head to her hands, Jordyn groaned. "Crayson, if you tell me you purchased the building right next door to my bar for your new cigar lounge, I will literally never speak to you again."

I shrug. "Not possible. We're in a wedding together, JayJay, so you have to talk to me. Plus, we're neighbors now."

"You've got to be shitting me," she yelled. "You really did purchase the building next door? Did you do that just to piss me off even more than you usually do?"

"Yes and no," I replied, trying to refrain from smiling again. I couldn't help it. Like I said, pissing off Jordyn was my favorite pastime.

"I can't believe this." She stood and started pacing the room. "I have a lot going on already, and the last thing I need is this shit." She stopped to glare at me. "Out of all of the buildings in Brooklyn, you had purchase one next to my bar! Don't you see anything wrong with that?"

"Not really."

She pointed a finger at me. "You're kidding, right? You don't think I deserved a heads-up?"

I clasped my hands together. "Not really."

"Or even a conversation beforehand that you were thinking of purchasing that space?"

"Not really."

"Ugh." She started pacing again. "If you say *not really* one more time, I'm gonna lose my shit."

Any person with a decent bone in their body would understand that now wasn't the moment to annoy someone. The right thing to do would be for me to leave her alone so she could process this news. A gentleman would excuse himself and give her some space. *Don't do it, Crayson. Don't egg her on more. Be a man about this.*

She shot me a stern look before sitting back down in the

chair she'd vacated. "Do you have anything to say for yourself?"

Her chest heaved up and down, and even though she was more pissed at me than usual, she still looked sexy as hell. *Shit. I have to say it.* "Not really."

"You asshole," she yelled, tossing a throw pillow at me.

I grunted. *Tell me something I don't know.*

THREE

Jordyn

"THAT NO GOOD, CHEATING ASS, STUPID ASS, UGLY ASS, dumb ass, still-lives-with-his-mama-ass, lousy excuse of a man."

I ground my teeth together as I stared at my ex-boyfriend and thought about all of the time I'd wasted on him. Looks wise, Luther wasn't actually ugly, but he might as well be since his personality sure was. And I'd heard he'd moved out of his mom's place a couple months ago. Not that I cared to keep tabs on him, but his mom still went to the same beauty salon that I went to, and in the salon, women talk. A little too much if you asked me.

"Tell me how you really feel," my girl Avery said as we both eyed the man who had put me through hell last year. Avery had never met him because she hadn't lived in New York yet, but she and I had done a lot of Facebook stalking over a bottle of tequila a couple months ago when I'd heard that his new wife was expecting twins.

"Out of all of the parties he could have attended, he had to show up to the one I was at." I crossed my arms over my chest as I watched him talk to another couple who was with him and his wife. "Look at him with that smug ass smirk and those shady ass eyes, probably over there talking out of his ass."

Avery placed a comforting hand on my arm. "Girl, you're better than this."

"Trifling ass," I mumbled.

"Sis, you've said the word *ass* about eight times already. And you know how frustrated you get when you go on these repetitive cursing binges. You're a few curse words away from yelling every word you can think of."

She was right. I could already feel my body temperature rising the longer I stared. I wasn't a virgin to cursing, and the moment I began saying the same curse word over and over, I was only a few minutes away from yelling every damn curse word I could think of.

It was a shame that some folks had a pre-conceived notion that women shouldn't curse like sailors. News flash: some women have a potty mouth. And although I appreciated my mom for literally washing my mouth out with soap when I was younger to try and instill those lady-like tendencies, the shit didn't work. Hell, if anything, it made me worse. I could curse a sailor under the table.

"Don't let that dick ruin your New Year's celebration."

I let her words sink in even though I was too caught up in my feelings to ignore Luther completely. His beady eyes kept glancing my way, so I knew he'd seen me. He was just ignoring me.

"And you look too good to let this fly red dress go to

waste, so do me a favor and find someone sexy to kiss at midnight to get your mind off your ex."

"Thanks, girl." After glaring in his direction for a few more seconds, I finally turned my back toward him and took a sip of my drink. That didn't mean I didn't have thoughts of breaking into his mama's place and chopping his balls off while he was sleeping, but at least I was able to appear to direct my attention elsewhere.

Avery raised her glass. "Let's make a toast."

I wasn't in the mood for a toast, but I knew my perky, glass-is-always-half-full friend wouldn't stop until I agreed. So, I slowly raised my glass.

"What are we toasting to?"

"To you, bitch," she said. "I have a feeling that this is going to be your year. I can feel it in my bones."

Apart from the impromptu trip to Colorado last week, I'd been so busy that I rarely went out anymore. Being a female bar owner in New York was one thing. Rebranding your bar in an industry that was constantly changing was another entity entirely. At thirty-one, I was the proud owner of Sweet Baby Jay's, a bar known for pairing unique drinks with tasty treats guaranteed to tease your pallet. But I didn't just fill your stomach with the unhealthy shit. I was all about organic ingredients, and although I'd only been in business for a few years, business was going extremely well.

However, it was time for me to incorporate one of my other loves into my business even more than I already did, and let's just say that my other love was a bit ... unconventional. So I hoped she was right. This was going to be my year.

"Where's Serenity and Ty?" I asked, glancing around the party.

"They're around here somewhere. As soon as Malakai

got here, he ran into a couple clients, so the two of them tagged along to do the whole schmoozing thing."

Reaching into my black clutch, I pulled out my iPhone. "Okay, there's thirty minutes until midnight, meaning I have to find a distraction before that."

Avery's eyes widened. "If we only have thirty minutes then I need to find Malakai ASAP. He lives ten minutes away, so we have to get moving."

I squinted my eyes in confusion. "Aren't you missing the point of sharing a kiss at the stroke of midnight if you leave now?"

"There's something else my fiancé and I would rather be doing at midnight if you know what I mean." Avery wiggled her eyebrows.

I laughed at her less than subtle facial expression. She'd been engaged to Malakai for such a short while, yet she couldn't contain her happiness. Even though she still lived in the same apartment complex as I did, she spent most of her time at his place. Already, instead of saying *me* or I, she was saying *we,* and although I pretended to gag at her cheesy-ness, I was so happy for her. "Bringing in the New Year by having sex? Okay, boo, I feel you."

Avery sighed. "There are a lot of things I'm anxious to feel and do tonight, and since I don't want to be arrested for indecent exposure, I guess I need to get moving."

We glanced around the room until we spotted Malakai and the others. Unfortunately, the other people with him weren't just Ty and Serenity, but rather an obnoxious Madden who I was less than thrilled to see. *Girl, you know that's not true.* As if the man in question knew I was thinking about him—or rather, trying not to think about him —his eyes met mine and a sexy smirk crossed his face.

"What the hell is he doing here?" I whispered to Avery

as we got closer to our friends. He was still wearing that sexy smirk, and judging by the playful look in his fuck-me eyes, his thoughts were anything but PG.

Avery rolled her eyes. "Are you seriously asking me why Malakai invited his brother to this New Year's Eve party?"

"Yes, bitch. That's exactly what I'm asking. You already know I can't stand Crayson Madden." I didn't need to elaborate. Anyone who knew Crayson knew that he was a lot of things ... Reckless things. Bad decision making things. Unfortunately, fine as hell was at the top of the list, although I'd never admit it out loud.

"Is this about last week?" Avery asked. I'd been mad as hell in Colorado when Crayson told me he'd purchased the building right next door to my bar. I was serious about my business, and the old Blackberry Restaurant building meant more to me than Crayson even knew. Granted, I knew someone would eventually buy it, but I'd even been saving up money to purchase it myself.

After I'd kicked him out of my room that night, I'd gone to find Avery so she could talk me off the cliff. She'd tried her best to make me see the bright side. Malakai had even jumped into the conversation to try and ease my worry. "Crayson may piss you off sometimes, but he's serious about his business. Maybe you both will find some common ground when he opens that location," he'd said.

This past year, I'd taken up meditation, but there wasn't enough calm in the world to keep me from strangling him that night. *Common ground? Common fucking ground? That was supposed to be comforting and make me forget the fact that I was going to have to see the one person who annoyed me to no end daily?* At least until he finished renovations. After that, my only hope was that he didn't stay at his Brooklyn location more than he had to.

"You know last week was fucked up," I huffed. "So, yeah. It's partially about his dumb ass purchase, and the other part is because like I said before, I can't stand his ass."

"Yeah, he was wrong for that move. He could have told you he was buying the building." She cocked her head in his direction. "But you'd be able to stand him a lot more if you let him knock out those cobwebs hanging from your vagina."

I gasped exaggeratedly as I placed my hand over my chest. "I'm gonna pretend like I didn't hear you say that. Lord knows I'm not letting that bonafide fuckboy anywhere near my vajajay." I lowered my voice since talking about him often made my voice carry. Whether that be from sexual frustration or denial of my attraction was my secret to keep.

Although I tried my best not to turn his way, I did. *Why does he have to look so good?* He was sporting a dark grey suit and white collared shirt that was undone at the top. As usual, he was wearing an expensive white gold watch— Cartier if I had to guess—that shined every time the light hit it. I knew it had to be white gold and not silver because Crayson never went cheap. Even when he rocked a plain white tee, it was usually Nike or Polo.

His hair was freshly cut, and I swore I'd never seen a man lined as precise as Crayson's fade was lined before I'd met him. He was rocking a beard when we'd first met, but last month he'd decided to go with the clean-shaven look. I'd always been a sucker for beards, until he walked in my bar donning a strong jawline that made his lips appear even more suckable than they had before.

And the asshole had the nerve to have a dimple! Not two dimples, just one sexy little one that made an appearance every time he smirked, and Crayson smirked a whole damn lot. *Quit daydreaming about him, Jordyn! Snap out of it!*

I shook my head before I told Avery, "Besides, he's not even my type."

Avery stopped dead in her tracks and turned to look at me. Her stop was so abrupt, I almost lost my footing in my red booties since she caught me off guard.

"What?" I asked. "You know how I feel about him."

"I know that he pisses you off and is annoying as hell, but I also know that the way you two bicker is like a twisted form of foreplay and you're attracted Crayson."

I shook my head. "Am not."

"Are too."

"Am not."

Avery crossed her arms over her chest. "So you're telling me that when Crayson smiles at you like you're the only woman in the room, or winks at you when he stops by the bar, that does nothing for you?"

I shrugged. "Nope."

Avery stepped closer to me. "What about those times when he compliments your outfit or is the first to notice a new haircut?"

Out of habit, I ran my hands over my chic haircut. I could rock a short cut as good as the next bitch, but it was always nice to get a compliment here and there.

"Maybe." I ignored her eye roll and continued walking to the group. I knew Avery was still watching me, and although I didn't really need to save face in front of my close friend, I was still in a bitchy mood after spotting my ex.

Just ignore him, I reminded myself. I knew he was gonna say something flirtatious to me because Crayson always had something flirty—or dirty—to say. *Always.*

FOUR

Jordyn

WHEN WE REACHED OUR GROUP OF FRIENDS, I COULD tell that everyone was waiting for Crayson and I to exchange words. Ever since Avery and Malakai had gotten together, the focus had switched to Crayson and I since it was no secret that he'd been trying to sleep with me since the day we met.

Although I'd grown to enjoy hanging out with our new crew, everybody was usually in everyone else's business. Crayson and I weren't business, but the way they acted sometimes, you would think we were. I assumed that it was the norm for groups of friends, but I'd always been more of a one-friend-at-a-time kind of girl. Yet, since meeting Avery and subsequently meeting everyone else, I was getting used to the group dynamic and camaraderie. Which meant, I should have been used to hanging around Crayson by now since his fine ass was always around.

I said a general, "Hey," to the group, making sure I avoided eye contact with Crayson. Didn't need that dude getting any unwanted ideas.

"Yass, bitch," Ty said, grabbing my hand and twirling me around. "You are slaying that red dress and heels."

"Thank you. Thank you." I did a cute little curtsey before telling him he looked good in his navy-blue suit and loafers. I didn't have to glance Crayson's way to know if he was looking. I looked damned good, so I knew he was.

Avery glanced at her watch before whispering into Malakai's ear. Two seconds later, they were saying their good-byes and rushing out of the party.

"Well damn," Serenity said. "They're running out of here like the place is on fire."

I looked at my friend and her fiancé, happy for her but feeling bad that my lady parts hadn't gotten any attention in longer than I cared to say. "If I had dick on demand like she did, I'd be rushing to get out of here, too." No sooner had the statement left my mouth did I realize my mistake.

"You could have dick on demand if you quit acting like you don't want it," Crayson remarked before he took a sip of his cognac. How did I know he was sipping cognac? Because every week he came into my bar, and every week he ordered the same thing ... Cognac on the rocks, little ice —only three cubes, four max, but who's counting—with a side of lime.

I waved him off as I turned back to the direction Avery and Malakai had just gone. "I'm not doing this with you tonight."

After a few seconds of him not saying anything, I turned back to face him. His smirk was still in place as he watched me over the top of his glass and took another sip of his drink.

Why is he always doing that? Why was he always trapping me with those deep amber eyes? My breath caught in my throat as I watched him battle between pulling me to him and kissing me senseless or strategizing on how to catch me in his fuckboy trap.

Not gonna happen, loverboy. I've played this game before and I have no interest in playing it again. Was Crayson sexy? Yeah. Was I long overdue for some male attention? Maybe. *Maybe? The answer is yes, bitch. Be honest with yourself!* However, what it came down to was simple. Was I willing to bend the promise I'd made to myself to never have sex with a man who changed women more than he changed his underwear? *Hell no.* I'd been there. Done that.

While Ty and Serenity continued the conversation they were having with Crayson before I showed up, I couldn't help but glance around the room again for my ex. My eyes landed on his lyin' ass and pregnant wife in the same spot they were before I'd joined my friends.

Case in point, I thought, observing the way Luther kept his hand on his wife's protruding belly while he smiled at the waitress in a way that was less than appropriate. *Luther is a player.* I'd known it the day we met. *And what does my dumb ass do? I decide to date him and even start making plans for our future and shit.* News flash: you can't plan a future with a man when you are just one out of ten women he's talking to. "

"What's putting that frown on your face, beautiful?"

I jumped at the sound of Crayson's voice and the way his breath was tickling my earlobe. It felt good. Too good. Yet, when I glanced over my shoulder, instead of telling him how I really felt, I said, "You're usually the cause of my frowns. So how do you know you didn't put this one here?"

He laughed in that deep drop-your-panties-for-me-right-now sort of way, but I kept the expression of indifference plastered on my face.

"That may be true, but I didn't put this one there." He adjusted himself so he was standing beside me and followed the direction of my eyes. "Do you know that couple?"

I sighed. "That man is my dumb ass ex. And that pregnant woman next to him is his wife, but also one of the women he was cheating on me with."

Crayson's eyebrows raised. "One of? You mean that bastard was cheating on you with multiple women?" His eyes swept my body up and down in appreciation, and I had to remind Diamond to calm the fuck down. Diamond was the name I'd given my pussy because why the hell were men only allowed to name their anatomy? Nah. That shit didn't sit well with me. Besides, Diamonds were a girl's best friends and every woman needed a ride or die bitch by her side.

Diamond was a rarity because good pussy was hard to find (and if you don't believe me, you betta ask somebody). She was a feisty bitch and a lot of men couldn't handle her. Hell, back in my early twenties, I'd had enough bad sex that I'd almost sewed *only real men need apply* on the crotch area of my favorite pair of jeans in bright pink sequins.

"He didn't deserve you." Crayson's voice broke through my thoughts, causing me to glance up at him despite my warning to myself not to. As usual, the gleam in his eyes caused my breath to catch. I glanced behind us in curiosity to look for our friends. At least, curiosity and not nervousness was what I was telling myself. The day I mentioned that Crayson Madden made me nervous would be the day that hell froze over.

"Where did Ty and Serenity go?"

"They both wanted to find someone to kiss before

midnight. They mentioned it aloud, but your attention was elsewhere."

Midnight ... I pulled out my iPhone again and glanced at the time. There were only two minutes until midnight. "I guess we should part ways and take our cue from them," I said, chancing a glance back at Crayson. As soon as my eyes met his, I'd wished I hadn't looked.

"We have a dilemma," he said, his eyes bouncing between my face and my lips. "Because the only person I want to kiss tonight is you."

I swallowed. "Why is that a dilemma?" *What the hell, Jordyn! Why did you ask that?*

His lips curled to the side in a smirk, and damned if that one dimple didn't do crazy things to Diamond. "The dilemma for you is the fact that you've told me multiple times that I'm the last person on this Earth you'd ever want to kiss."

My usual snarky remark got caught in my throat because he wasn't lying. That's what I *said*, but that wasn't the whole truth.

"For me, my dilemma is that I'd never kiss a woman who didn't want to be kissed by me." He stepped closer. "So if what you've been saying for months is true, I'll do as you wish and let you find someone else to kiss tonight." He brought his head to my right ear. "Or, you can get back at your ex who hasn't been able to take his eyes off you all night, and show him that although he did you wrong, you're thriving and aren't fazed by him being there."

I kept my head in place when I replied, "And how would I do that? How would I show him I'm thriving and unbothered?" Even before Crayson responded, I was pretty sure I knew the answer.

"Let me kiss you," he whispered. "For tonight. In this

moment. Forget how much you hate me and ignore the fact that you're well aware I want to fuck you into next Sunday. Just for tonight, give me the honor of kissing those pretty plush lips and making your ex jealous." My breath hitched, but he wasn't done yet. "And by lips, I was referring to the ones on your beautiful face, but if you're feeling bold tonight, I could kiss your other pair, too."

I mentally slapped my hand against my forehead. *Damn.* He was so crass, and unfortunately, I loved that shit. His naughty words turned me on even though I wished they didn't.

I took a few seconds to contemplate what he was suggesting. *You shouldn't do it. Tell his ass no like you always do.* However, instead of telling him to get lost, I found myself admitting that, "I hate New Year's Eve because I'm not fond of kissing at midnight or any other night. It's sloppy, unpredictable, and a lot of men can't do it right."

It was true. I'd never liked kissing. Yet, telling Crayson was the wrong thing to do. I didn't even know why I told him that in the first place, but him being this close was messing with my reasoning skills. He'd take it as a challenge. Duh!

I turned my head in an attempt to tell him I wasn't interested like I should have said the moment he began whispering in my ear. However, instead of me declining his tempting offer, I was rendered speechless when he tilted his head to mine and captured my lips, while his arms snaked around my waist, pulling me closer to him.

In a perfect world, I would have pushed him away and said he had no business kissing me like that. In my world, one of my hands went to the back of his head, holding him in place, while the other landed on his hard chest.

Holy shit. The man kissed me in slow, lazy strokes as if we had all of the time in the world. As if it wasn't a small miracle that we were here, in this moment, after all of the times I'd told him I wasn't interested.

Crayson deepened the kiss, his tongue stroking mine in a way I'd never felt before. He tasted of Cognac, and although I wasn't a fan of the liquor, kissing him was making me a fan. I could get drunk off his lips.

Oh my God, what is he doing to me? It was true what I'd said. I'd never enjoyed kissing that much. But clearly, I'd been messing with the wrong dudes because Crayson knew what the hell he was doing. He knew damn well he was kissing me senseless. It was so good. *Too good.*

When my better sense kicked in, I ended the kiss and took a much-needed step back. I looked around the room at everyone cheering and celebrating, and realized he must have kissed me at midnight. Either that, or he'd kissed me before and I missed the damn countdown.

I glanced in the direction of my ex in time to catch him eyeing me with a pissed off expression on his face. *Serves your ass right!* He needed a small taste of his own medicine even if I wasn't his anymore.

Speaking of *his*, I was scared to even look in Crayson's direction because he'd owned every part of me during that kiss and I still hadn't recovered. Yes, a bitch was truly alarmed and I wasn't afraid to admit that because any woman who'd been avoiding a man for months, only to find out that he could kiss like he was making sweet love to your mouth, would understand why my heart was beating out of my chest.

You see, Crayson was the type of man who you needed to keep in a wrought iron box. As long as he was in that box with no tools, he couldn't get out. However, the minute you gave in to the humane side of you and gave him a torch, he'd burn through that box in minutes.

In this case, my lips had been the torch, and when I finally did chance a glance at him, the gleam I saw in his eyes had Diamond doing somersaults, while I, on the other hand, was freaking the hell out. He didn't even have to speak for me to know what he was thinking, but true to Crayson's style, he couldn't not speak. He just had to say something to make me even more anxious.

"You know what you just did?" he asked.

Don't play his game, I warned myself. I didn't even know why I'd warned myself, because I knew I was too curious not to ask him, "What?"

The sly smile that filled his face told me everything. "You just fucked up," he replied. "Because now that I know how good you taste, there's no way I'm not tasting you again." His eyes roamed over me. "And next time, I don't plan on just stopping at your mouth."

I averted my eyes, but it was no use—the damage had already been done. So the main question I had to ask myself was, *How in the world am I going to avoid him when he's opening a business right next door?*

The answer lingered in my mind like a blinking neon light. There would be no avoiding Crayson Madden, and any woman—myself included—who felt differently was in for a rude awakening.

FIVE

One month later ...

Crayson

IT WAS EARLY IN THE MORNING AND MALAKAI HAD offered to help me get some things situated now that my Brooklyn cigar lounge was taking formation.

Since my Manhattan location was called Unclassified Hideaway, and my location in Queens was called Unsettled Retreat, I'd decided to call my Brooklyn lounge Undefined Sanctum. However, this location would have the most exclusivity, as a members-only lounge targeting a certain type of middle-class and affluent clientele.

Many would think my Manhattan location would be the most distinct and high-class, but I didn't like to do what people expected. Folks didn't have to understand my decisions, but they damn sho' needed to respect them.

"I hope you realize that you're a dead man walking if

you keep this shit up," my brother, Malakai, said, breaking my thoughts.

I looked up from the box I was unpacking. "I don't what you're talking about."

"You know what I'm talking about." He stopped the box he was unpacking and walked over to me. "For the past month, you've managed to piss off Jordyn more than usual. What's with you?"

I kept unpacking, not ready to answer his question because it would make me sound like a whiny bitch. What Malakai was saying was true. I'd been annoying Jordyn more than usual, and the fact that she couldn't get rid of me since I was renovating the building right next door to her bar, had her cursing my ass out on a daily basis.

After that explosive kiss we'd shared on New Year's Eve, she'd gone right back to the old Jordyn, opting to pretend it didn't happen and avoid me whenever she could. I wasn't one of those sensitive ass niggas by any means, but I hadn't been able to get her out of my mind after that kiss. So, to see her brush it off like it meant nothing had hurt a little. *Fuck, I am a sensitive asshole.* What was even crazier than feeling butt hurt, was the fact that I hadn't had sex since the kiss I'd shared with Jordyn.

Oh trust me, I'd had plenty of pussy thrown my way lately, but every time I thought about taking a sexy ass hunny home, Jordyn would consume my mind. Therefore, what did I do every time I saw her? Anything I could to annoy her, which may or may not have included telling this dude she had a little crush on who frequents her bar that she batted for the other team and was still in the closet. Who knew his lame ass would tell her?

"You do realize that unless one of you sells their property, you both will be stuck next door to each other for a very long time, right?"

I shrugged. "What's your point??

"My point is, it would do you some good to dial back your asshole-ish ways and try and be cool to Jordyn so you both can run your businesses in harmony."

"I tried to talk to her," I said honestly. "But she won't even give me a minute of her time."

"Did you try apologizing for how you've been treating her lately?"

I lifted an eyebrow. "Me apologize? For what, annoying her?"

Malakai shook his head. "Yes, that's exactly what I mean."

"News flash, bruh, I annoy folks all the time. And you seem to forget that Jordyn isn't going around apologizing to me for all those months of cursing me out before I even got a word in."

"Man, please, you know you like that shit. You always had a thing for classy Christians who be in the club before church every Sunday sayin' 'I love Jesus, but I curse a little.' And by a little, I mean a damn lot!"

I laughed harder than I should have, but I couldn't help it. My brother definitely knew my type and Jordyn fit that description to a T. The more she yelled, the more I wanted her. The more she cursed, the more I imagined her sexy mouth wrapped around my dick, shutting her up. I know, I know. I'm a sick bastard.

"You could be right." As bad as it sounded, I'd never thought about apologizing to Jordyn for always doing shit to piss her off. I also hadn't banked on her being even more annoyed with me than usual after I made up that white lie to that I-wear-a-suit-everyday-so-people-know-I-make-money stuffy ass nigga so he wouldn't ask her out.

I took a break from unpacking the box of supplies I'd ordered online as I thought about how busy I'd been this past month. Opening a new location was no joke, and when I wasn't bothering Jordyn, I was juggling my time between my other two locations and the new property.

When I'd purchased this property for my new cigar lounge, I knew it was a good investment. Like Jordyn's building, the lower level was functional for a business and two floors above were four apartments. I'd already made some updates to the apartments, making the three current tenants very happy that I was their new owner. I'd never met the fourth tenants because the newlywed couple had moved out a week before I purchased the property, so I'd decided to turn it into a hospitality suite for my elite customers, which meant, when it wasn't occupied, I was able to stay there instead of going to my condo in Harlem.

"Maybe I should just apologize and see if we can start over," I finally said.

"There's no way in hell you can get a fresh start," Malakai replied with a laugh. "Jordyn isn't the type to forgive and forget. But there's a chance that your apology would make her consider calling it a truce."

I gave him a questioning look. "A truce to what?"

"A lot of things." Malakai pointed to the wall my lounge shared with her bar. "Case in point, you had one of your main surround sound speakers placed on this wall when you know Jordyn's office is right on the other side of the speaker."

I gave an innocent shrug. "I didn't remember where her office was."

Malakai laughed. "Save your bullshit for someone who

hasn't known you since you were born." He glanced around the cigar lounge that was nowhere close to being done, but you could see the potential. "I'm proud of you, little brother." He clasped my shoulder. "But it's time for you to grow the fuck up."

"Tell me what's good then, bruh," I said with a laugh. "You've always known I fuck shit up."

He nodded his head. "Yeah, that's true. But fucking shit up and being a fuck up are two different things." He waved his hands around the room. "You're opening your third lounge, so I'd say you've proven to anyone who ever doubted you that you're not a fuck up. So stop fucking with Jordyn. She's my fiancée's best friend and we need y'all both to get along for the sake of our wedding."

At his words, it dawned on me where his brotherly advice was coming from. Malakai was no newbie to dealing with my bullshit, but his soon-to-be wife was. "Did Avery tell you to check my ass so our bickering wouldn't ruin your wedding?"

Malakai looked around as if Avery would pop up any minute. In hindsight, it could happen since she was next door at Jordyn's bar. "I'm not at liberty to say if she told me to talk to you about it or not. But for argument's sake, let's just say that she did warn me that I had to get a certain best man of mine to stop bothering her maid of honor for the sake of our impending wedding, you would understand why I would be obligated to talk to you, right?"

I chuckled as I said, "Happy wife, happy life. I get it. I'll try to dial back my inner asshole for the sake of your relationship."

Malakai smiled. "I knew you would understand, brother. I only ask that you try to take it down a notch."

I nodded as we got back to work. I still had a lot more to

do and not a lot of time to do it if I wanted the place to be ready for Malakai and Avery's engagement party and my grand opening. Halfway through cleaning my newly installed counters, I had a thought.

"JORDYN, ARE YOU SURE YOU AREN'T OVERDOING IT with the cupcake frosting?"

I looked from the random spot on the wall I'd been staring at and turned to Avery. "What do you mean?"

My eyes followed her line of vision as she pointed to the red velvet cupcake I was decorating. "Oh, shit." I put down my pipe bag filled with cream cheese frosting and sighed. I'd covered it so much, you couldn't even tell it was a cupcake anymore.

"I'm sorry," I said, before scooping some of the frosting off the cupcake. "I don't know where my mind was at." The bold-faced lie left my lips easily and my only hope was that Avery wouldn't push me too much on what was wrong with me.

After waking up as the sun rose, I'd called Avery and asked if she could come to my apartment since I was taking a much-needed break from being in my bar today. Like a true friend, she'd sensed something was wrong and stopped over right after the sun had come up.

Now that she was here, I wished I hadn't called. I thought I was ready to talk to her about what had been going on with me, but I wasn't.

Her concerned eyes were staring a hole in me when she asked, "What's wrong, Jordyn? You're worrying me."

"I'm fine," I replied, getting my ingredients ready to decorate another cupcake. "I shouldn't have called you earlier this morning. I was just feeling a bit overwhelmed about my bar."

Part of that was true. I really was overwhelmed with what I'd been doing at the bar lately, but there were other things going on as well.

"You got up to bake at 4 a.m. and you're only decorating one cupcake at a time," she pointed out. "A clear sign that everything is not okay."

Damn, she knows me too well. "I just haven't been getting enough sleep." She squinted her eyes as if she didn't believe me. I tried to ease her suspicion when I said, "Something is bothering me. I thought I was ready to talk about it, but I'm not. You being here is making all the difference and I promise to talk to you when I'm ready."

She relaxed her face, supposedly satisfied with my words. "Can you just tell me if it has anything to do with Crayson being a pain in your ass lately?"

I frowned. "He's such an asshole, but what I'm going through has nothing to do with him."

"Good. Because Malakai is with him right now and I told him to talk to Crayson about the way he treats you."

"I'm sure that conversation is going well," I said with a laugh. "Crayson will deny that he's even being more annoying than usual."

Avery swiped one of the cupcakes I'd just decorated. She took a big bite, before telling me, "He's a man-child. He's like the boy in school who instead of telling a girl he likes her, pulls her pigtails and trips her on the way to recess."

I laughed harder than I had in days because what she said was true. He was a man-child. "In his defense, I've been in a pissy mood this past month, too."

Avery lifted her mouth to the side in a way that I knew

meant she wanted to ask me something, but was trying to figure out how to broach the topic.

We'll be sitting in silence forever if she doesn't just ask me whatever it is. "Spit it out."

She shrugged. "Nothing to spit out."

"Girl, please. You've been giving me the Bambi eyes for a few minutes."

"Did anything happen between you and Crayson that you haven't told me?" she spurted out.

My eyes widened. "Um, no. Why would you think that?" I hadn't told anyone about the toe-curling kiss I'd shared with Crayson because, in all honesty, none of our friends could keep a secret. At first, I was waiting to see if Crayson said something to Malakai because then I knew he would say something to Avery and she would, in turn, tell me that word of our kiss was out before getting on my ass about not telling her first.

Instead, none of that had happened. So as much as I'd wanted to tell Avery about the kiss and ask her if I was insane for locking lips with a man I claimed to hate, I'd enjoyed the fact that it was our little secret.

"I think you're lying, but I won't push you on it."

I smiled and continued to decorate the remaining cupcakes as we discussed Avery's wedding plans so far. While she spoke, my mind kept drifting to Crayson and it wasn't because we were both standing up in our friend's wedding or had shared a kiss that I doubt would ever be topped by another man. Nope. My mind was on him for other reasons. Business reasons. And whether I wanted to or not, I had to talk to him and explain why I'd been so pissed about him buying the property next door. He may think it only had to do with the fact that we rarely got along, but that wasn't the only reason.

You have to put on your big girl panties, Jordyn. You have to talk to him because you need to work together on this. I wanted to groan aloud at that realization, but I didn't want to interrupt Avery's play-by-play on her and Malakai's meeting with the event coordinator at the venue they'd chosen. *Shit.* I hadn't relied on someone in a long time, yet, in order to move forward with my business plan, I needed to rely on Crayson ... even if it was only in a small way.

Before I was finished topping the last cupcake with sprinkles, I'd made my mind up. I'd talk to Crayson about the part of my business that I'd never shared with anyone before and hope like hell that he understood why I needed us to work together.

SIX

Crayson

"Shit," I cursed as I accidently hammered my right hand. Although I wasn't a contractor, I was very good at building things. If I hadn't opened my cigar lounge chain, I would have had my own construction firm instead.

Even though I was usually very focused when I worked, I couldn't focus today. I hadn't been sleeping well ever since my conversation with Malakai a couple days ago and I couldn't figure out why it had bothered me.

You know why, the voice inside of my head taunted. *You regret the way you've acted to Jordyn lately.* It was no secret that I could be a pain in the ass, but I'd be the first to admit that I'd been worse than usual. I knew if I didn't talk to her and apologize, it would keep fucking with my work.

"Are you okay?"

I turned to the front door, surprised to see Jordyn standing there with a tray of desserts. *Damn, she looks good.*

Despite being next door, we hadn't seen much of each other this week.

She placed the tray on the counter and removed her black pea coat and infinity scarf. Today, she was wearing jeans, tall, black boots, and a graphic tee that read *Bitches Never Quit*. I smiled because the shirt was just like Jordyn.

"Did you hear me?" she asked.

That's right. She asked me a question when she walked in.

"I went a little too far right and hit my hand with the hammer."

She frowned before she stepped closer to me "Asshole, you have to be careful."

I laughed at her not-so-endearing term. It took a particular kind of skillset to be able to say a curse word as if it were someone's legal name. When she reached me, she held out her hand and it took me a few moments to figure out that she wanted me to place my injured hand in hers.

I barely gave myself permission to breathe as I stood there while she inspected the injury. I didn't want to ruin the moment since I was still surprised she was even touching me at all.

Her touch feels good. She caressed my hand as if it were as delicate as a dainty flower, even though I had the calluses and rough patches as proof that it wasn't.

"You'll live," she said, dropping my hand. "Nothing's broken."

"Thanks." My hand missed her touch already, which was ridiculous since nothing about her touch had been intimate. But my mind didn't work that way. One innocent touch from Jordyn and I was already having images of placing her on top of the counter and opening her legs to allow me to stand between them. I'd start kissing her first.

Slowly, just like I did on New Year's. Then, I'd move from her lips to her neck, lightly suckling the spot right behind her earlobe, relishing in the soft moans she'd make as my tongue got to work.

Crayson, snap out of it, that voice said. *You need to clear the air with Jordyn, not think about kissing her again.* Clearing my throat, I placed my hands in the pocket of my jeans so that I wouldn't be tempted to reach out and touch her.

I sat down and motioned for her to sit in the chair opposite of me. "I've been meaning to talk to you about something." I cleared my throat again. "I want to apologize for how I've been treating you since we met, but especially this past week."

She squinted her eyes and crossed her hands over her chest like she didn't believe me, so I continued. "Jordyn, you already know I'm attracted to you, and even if you didn't feel it that night, I enjoyed our kiss more than I ever expected I would. Everything felt right about that moment. So after New Year's, when you decided to ignore me and act like it didn't happen, it hurt a little."

Her face softened. "Most men wouldn't be able to admit that a woman had hurt their feelings."

My lips curled to the side in a smile. "I'm not most men." And it would do her some damn good if she remembered that because although I was apologizing, that didn't mean I'd changed my mind about sleeping with her. Chemistry this strong was too rare to go to waste. Sometimes, two people just needed to hash it out between the sheets. I know some say that talking solves everything, but I tend to disagree. Talking may help, but great sex helped even more.

She frowned. "Why are you still smiling like that?"

"No reason," I said. "Just hoping you realize that even

though I apologized for being an asshole, that doesn't mean I won't fuck you into next week when you finally realize that we'd be damn good together."

"Ha!" she huffed. "I don't know where your dick has been, but I know it's not coming anywhere near me."

I was shaking my head before she'd even finished her statement. "Sooner or later, you'll let me fuck you. It's just a matter of when and where."

"And the asshole is back," she muttered, standing from her chair. "Luckily for you, I came here to talk to you about something important, so I'll chew your ass out later for not talking to me like a fucking lady."

I chuckled. *Did she hear herself?* "You came to see me for an important reason?" I sat back in my chair "Now I'm intrigued." I expected her to have another snarky comment, but instead, she seemed nervous. *That's new.* Jordyn rarely looked nervous about anything.

She picked up the tray of desserts and placed it on the square table in between our two chairs. I reached out to grab one of the cookies, and she slapped my hand away.

"What gives? I thought you brought these for me?"

"I did, but you have to let me explain something first." She sighed. "I can't believe you're the first person I'm telling this to who knows my real identity."

Real identity? I quirked an eyebrow. "What exactly do you have to tell me?"

Instead of answering me, she handed me a sheet of paper and a pen. "I need you to sign this before we talk any further."

I opened the folded paper and read the first few lines before my eyes flew to hers. "A non-disclosure agreement? You want me to sign an NDA?"

"Yes," she replied. "I need you to sign it. I need to be

able to trust you."

Now I was even more confused. "According to you, you hate my guts. And I recall you telling me that you wouldn't even trust me if your life depended on it."

She cringed. "Okay, so maybe I was being a little dramatic at the time."

"A little? You also turned to Avery one time and told her to have you admitted to a mental hospital the day you'd allow yourself to think I was a decent man worthy of laying an unwanted hand on you."

"I get your point," she said, stretching out her hands. "But I'm asking you to sign this because I meant what I said. I really need to talk to you."

I wanted to know what she had to say, so I skimmed the NDA, signed it, and handed it back to her. She looked relieved that I'd signed it and put it away in her purse. I thought she'd jump right into what she wanted to talk about, but she studied me some more, so I let her observe me, hoping whatever she found indicated she could trust me.

She kept me waiting a couple more minutes until finally, she took a deep breath and looked me square in the eyes. I found myself holding my breath in the process. "Crayson Madden," she said, her voice firm. Precise. Very business-like. "You may know me as Jordyn Jameson, but there are quite a few folks in New York who know me as Shay Sinclair."

I scrunched my eyes together. "So your name isn't Jordyn Jameson?"

"It is," she said. "Shay is a pseudonym."

"Why do you need a pseudonym?"

She smiled, but it wasn't one of those endearing smiles. Nor was it one of those cute, flirty smiles. This smile was stern, as if it held secrets that she wouldn't dare tell even though she clearly had something she needed to tell me. "You're looking at the brain behind the largest organic edible business in the state of New York," she said.

Edible business? Call me slow, but it was taking my brain a little while to catch up. "By edibles, do you mean ..."

"Marijuana." she clarified. "For seven years, I've been baking, creating, and selling delicious edibles in New York. My ingredients are all organic, and according to some of my top customers, the taste is outstanding. What started off small is now an entire empire." Her voice got lower as she leaned toward me. "And you, my dear asshole, got in the way of expanding my business exactly five weeks ago."

She sat back in her chair, crossed her legs, and clasped her hands in her lap. I didn't see a hint of the nervousness I'd previously seen when she said, "You may want to fuck me, but in a way, you already have." She held my gaze, and although I wanted to say something, I was speechless. "You should know that I don't fuck with my money," she said. "So it seems to me like you and I have an issue, and I *hate* having issues when it comes to business."

I swallowed a few times, sure that my Adam's apple looked like a damn bobble head. But I wasn't swallowing because I was nervous. True, the way she was speaking made me feel like two muscled security guards were going to approach at any moment and give me a good ass whooping if I said something wrong, but I wasn't worried about that. I was more shocked than anything.

In that moment, gone was my soon-to-be-sister-in-law's best friend who was hesitant to trust me and avoided my advances. She'd been replaced by this sexy siren who was much more of a boss bitch than I'd ever given her credit for.

I was the one in my family who'd been in more trouble than I cared to recount. I was the one everyone deemed the fuck-up. The one who'd made something of himself despite having all of the cards stacked against him. I was the one who'd gone to county jail more than a few times, until I'd had a heart-to-heart with my dad about getting my shit together before I ended up being a statistic and in prison like so many other young black men.

Yet, here I was, staring at a beautiful, feisty woman who'd starred in all my naughty fantasies lately, and she was telling me that she was more dangerous than I'd ever been. I was no damn angel and would never claim to be. But Jordyn? Jordyn was making me feel like a fucking saint. A goddamn Mother Theresa compared to whatever the hell she was into. She was running a weed operation, and whether she'd call it that or not, that's exactly how I saw it.

I ran my fingers down my face as I tried to make sense of everything she'd told me. I wasn't a virgin to the law, so I was pretty damn sure her business wasn't legal.

"What are you thinking?" she asked after several minutes of silence.

What am I thinking? I was thinking a whole lot of shit, but I didn't even know how to verbalize everything going on in my mind right now. So, I said the first thought I could formulate. The first thought that kept placing itself at the forefront of my brain.

"This shit sounds unreal." I watched her shift in her chair, but her face didn't give away any sign that she was uncomfortable. "You'll have to elaborate on how I'm messing with your money, but I will warn you, that if you thought telling me you're an organic drug dealer would make me back off, you're mistaken." I leaned closer to her, glad to see her breath catch, breaking a little bit of her cool. "I've always known you were a bad bitch, so if anything, I want to fuck you even more now." And that was real talk.

SEVEN

Jordyn

AN ORGANIC DRUG DEALER? I'D NEVER THOUGHT OF IT that way, but clearly, Crayson did. Based off the way he was eye fucking me, I'd even dare to say he liked what he'd heard.

I'd imagined this moment a lot over the past few weeks, but never would I have thought our chemistry would be even more potent than usual after telling him a secret I vowed to never tell any of our friends.

There were only two things that I often thought that people needed to know about me. One, I was nobody's bitch and if you screwed me over, eventually, you'd get yours. My ex had his coming and the verdict was still out on Crayson since we had a lot more to discuss.

Two, the shit that all those horoscopes said about Geminis was true. I definitely had two personalities. In the case of this conversation I'd started with Crayson, I'd walked into his cigar lounge as Jordyn, but now, he was meeting Shay. Granted, Jordyn and Shay were the same person, but Shay operated differently than Jordyn.

Jordyn was the bar owner who baked tasty desserts that paired nicely with the wine, beer, and spirits she carried in her bar. Shay, on the other hand, had built an edibles empire by creating delicious treats laced in weed, guaranteed to tease your pallet and get you high in a different way than liquor did.

I was proud of both businesses, but there was no way I could run both and keep my sanity if I didn't compartmentalize. Doing so had made me more successful in both industries than I'd ever imagined. However, I also wasn't naïve enough to think what I was doing wasn't dangerous. I'd already learned that it was, but I'd been through my fair share of shit in life, so there wasn't much that I wasn't prepared for.

"Is what you're doing legal?" he asked.

I shook my head. "Medical marijuana became legal a few years ago, but recreational use in the state of New York isn't legalized yet. It's getting there, though, and I'm sure you know other states like Maine, California, and Colorado have legalized recreational use."

I could see the questions beginning to formulate in Crayson's mind, and although I wanted him to understand why I'd gone into this business, I didn't want to dive into everything. Getting too deep into the *when did I get into this* and *how did I get into this* would force me to have to try and explain *why did I get into this*. I wasn't ready to explain why I'd started this business just yet.

"I know you have a lot of questions, but I need to tell you what your business has in common with mine."

He gave me a confused look. "I guess I can see what

cigars and weed have in common since you smoke both, but I'm confused on the business thing."

I shook my head. "I don't go on street corners selling weed."

"I didn't say you did."

"But you were thinking it." He didn't deny it, so I continued by telling him, "Being in the edibles business means just what it sounds like. I lace all of the tasty treats I bake with marijuana, and my clientele are not the type who are on street corners trying to find the next dealer to give them a hit. That's not what I do. That's not who they are."

"Okay, I believe you." His eyes studied mine. "So, what do you have to discuss with me that has to do with my cigar lounge?"

I sighed, mentally giving myself a pep talk to dive into the rest of this conversation by asking, "Did you know the owner of Blackberry Restaurant before he passed? Mr. Briggs?"

He shook his head. "I knew him a little. Why?"

"I knew he wanted to retire by the end of last year, so he and I had talked business. He was going to sell me his restaurant. But before I could do that, he passed away suddenly. I'd just gone to his funeral a couple weeks before I went to Colorado, the same trip in which you told me you brought the place. Which didn't make sense because it wasn't for sale."

"I know his grandson, Stephen," Crayson said. "We played ball together in some pick-up games a few years back and we kept in touch. He and his wife live in Florida now and he contacted me when Mr. Briggs passed away. Said he needed to sell the place quickly and I mentioned that I was researching properties to open my third cigar lounge, Undefined Sanctum. The rest fell into place."

So he wasn't buying the place as some messed up way to get close to me. "Why didn't you tell me that you didn't actively seek to get close to me?"

He cleared his throat. "Honestly?"

"Honestly," I repeated.

"Before Stephen had contacted me, I'd been looking at the property one block over. A part of me wanted to open my first Brooklyn lounge, and you're in a great location. Another part of me felt like finding a place closer to your bar wouldn't hurt since that meant I'd get to see you more."

His words should have annoyed me, but they didn't. I appreciated his honesty, but I still had a problem. "Come on, I have to show you something." Rising from the chair, I motioned for him to follow me as I walked to the stairs that led to the basement. I cut on the light and began walking down.

"Hold up," he said at the top of the stairs. "This isn't where you trap me downstairs, cut my dick off, and bury me alive where no one will ever find me, is it?"

I frowned. "If I was trying to kill you, why would I cut your dick off first? Why not just kill you and get it over with?"

Crayson glanced at where we were just sitting. "I'm sorry, but did you not just sit me down for what I thought was going to be simple conversation, but instead, you tell me you're the biggest organic drug dealer in New York? If you ever kill a guy, no doubt you're cutting off his dick." His face grew serious. "Wait! Have you ever killed anyone?"

"What?" I yelled. "Of course not! How could you even think that?" I hit him on his shoulder and was met with solid muscle.

"Just asking," he said with a shrug. "So you're not a murderer. Just an organic drug dealer then."

"Ugh," I groaned. "Stop calling me a drug dealer."

"Okay, female drug lord."

"Eww. No! I hate that."

"Drug kingpin."

"Would you stop saying the word drug! Marijuana isn't a drug."

He laughed. "Why don't you ask the police force of New York if they'd agree with you on that."

I placed my hands on my hips. "Please stop with the crappy nicknames. You're not good at it."

Ignoring what I said, he placed his hand on his chin as if he was giving this a lot of thought. "Would Marijuana Queenpin work better?"

I shook my head. "You're an idiot. Just follow me and I promise it will make sense soon." I had to hold in my nervous laugh because, quite frankly, there was nothing to laugh about. All his nicknames painted me out to be a drug dealer. "I should slap you across the back of your head for disrespecting me with those obnoxious nicknames."

I briefly turned to look up at him as we descended the stairs. His cocky smile was still in place, so I should have known he was going to say something like, "The only way I'm letting you slap me is if you give me the honor of bending you over this railing to slap that juicy ass of yours."

And just like that, the heat flowing between us was reignited, even though I wasn't sure it had ever been put out in the first place. "We're here," I said, approaching in the back of the basement, farthest to the left.

"Nice," Crayson remarked. "I can totally see why you wanted to bring me to this nice white wall."

Ignoring his sarcasm, I dove into my explanation. "Mr. Briggs was actually a friend of my grandfather's," I said. "That's how I'd found out about the property next door being for sale. I grew up in Maine and my family still lives there, but originally, my grandfather is from New York. He and Mr. Briggs kept in touch, so I reached out to him when I moved here over seven years ago. Two years after that, I purchased my bar."

Crayson nodded his head. "You said you'd been in the edibles business for seven years, so you did that first."

"Yes, I did," I stated, surprised he'd remember how long I'd been in business given everything else we'd discussed.

"It's a small world. I didn't know Steven's dad well, but I also wasn't aware we both knew the Briggs family."

"Mr. Briggs was a great business neighbor," I said. "But I realized after five years, my bar and business were expanding and I was running out of space. I thought I would have to move into a bigger location, but then he told me he was selling. However, that wasn't what sold me."

"I assume you brought me down here because the basement is what sold you?" Crayson glanced around the space. "Although I have no idea why since it seems pretty ordinary."

"It is ordinary." I glanced around to look for something I could use to break through the dry wall and found a metal pipe. "Do you trust me?"

He looked from my eyes to the pipe in my hand. "I'm pretty sure I should say no, but I'm going to go with yes, I trust you."

With all the strength I had, I used the metal pipe to bust a hole through the wall.

"What the fuck are you doing?" Crayson grabbed my hand after the second swing, but it didn't matter. I'd already done what I wanted to do.

"Have you lost your mind?" he asked me.

"Not yet." I glanced through the hole, happy to see it

was precisely as I'd hoped. "Did you ever wonder why this side of the room has been cut off?" I pointed to where the wall protruded out. "It doesn't cover the same square footage as the levels above. It's the same way in my bar. Mr. Briggs had stopped over one day and told me that between this property and mine, there are stairs leading to a grand room even farther underground that him and the previous owner discovered years ago. Apparently, it was built during the prohibition period when it was illegal to sell alcohol. So they stored it underground."

"You're shitting me," he said, looking through the hole like I had. "I can't believe it's a piece of history connecting our properties."

"Me neither. Especially since, for now, it's just the kind of expansion I need. Plus, it's private."

He stood back up. "Wait, you know how big the space is?"

"Yep. I made a bigger opening than this into this space, but I can't see completely down the stairs and into the room. But Mr. Briggs said it was large enough to fit a hundred people. I hid the hole behind the large artwork hanging on my wall."

Crayson glared. "Why didn't you just take me to your bar and show me this since you've already broken though your wall?"

I smiled. "And miss the expression on your face when you thought I was going to destroy your basement? Never."

He shook his head. "I guess I had that one coming." He looked back toward the hole in the wall. "So, I'm guessing you want to be able to use this room and only told me because half of it goes into my property."

"Exactly," I said. "A very elite client of mine has put in a huge order of five thousand edibles that my team and I have to fulfill. Most of the work is being done in my warehouse, but my warehouse isn't located in New York. It's in Maine. So I need this space to prepare and store as much as I can, and I only have a few weeks to get it done and delivered by the deadline. Plus, some of the edibles are unique to my personal recipes and I refuse to share it. I have to deliver the first batch of one-thousand in a week. So it's all hands on deck."

"Five-thousand," Crayson muttered. "Who the hell is your client?"

I did a motion of zipping my lips. "Can't tell you that. Client confidentiality. But I can say that it will be extremely bad for business if I don't deliver. So what do you say? Can you keep my secret and are you okay with me utilizing this space?"

"You made me sign an NDA," he reminded. "But even if you hadn't, I'd keep your secret. I could even help you create a doorway for the secret room to help you out. Can't have you pissing off these rich clients of yours."

My eyes widened in surprise. "I can't ask you to do that."

"You didn't ask," he said. "Plus, that's my request. I'll let you use the space for whatever you want and even block off my basement so that I'm the only one allowed down here when I'm staffed, but in return, you have to let me help you fulfill this order by helping you in any way I deem fit."

He must be joking. I hadn't gotten to where I was by letting people take my control away. I'd already gone through a period in my life when I didn't have control of anything, so there was no way I was going through that again.

Crayson must have sensed my hesitancy because he said, "I promise that if you tell me I'm in the way of you fulfilling your order, I'll step aside and let you work without me distracting you."

I relaxed a little, confident that he was telling me the truth. The businesswoman in me wanted to draw up another contract to get his words down in writing. However, I knew that was Shay talking. Shay didn't take anyone for their word. Shay made sure that everything was trackable and recorded. Shay would demand that Crayson not make any more promises until she could draw up an additional contract.

"Okay, it's a deal." Clearly, Shay was no longer in charge where Crayson was concerned.

EIGHT

Crayson

I woke up the next morning with my mind still reeling over everything Jordyn had told me yesterday. I'd confirmed that none of our friends knew about her edibles business, including her best friend, Avery. I didn't know what I'd done in life to be the lucky bastard who got to know one of the biggest secrets in Jordyn Jameson's life, but I was damn glad it was me and not some other guy.

And she's so badass she has an entire team. After we'd placed a few boxes I'd stored in the basement in front of the hole to cover it, we'd gone back upstairs where I'd asked Jordyn a few more questions. She hadn't answered most of them, which had been fine with me. If I was in her shoes, I probably wouldn't have answered them either.

I'd learned so much about her over the past twenty-four hours. Needless to say, I was even more impressed by Ms. Jameson than I had been before. Since today was

Sunday, I knew she'd gone to church and was back by now. I should call first, but I just wanted to see her. Had to see her.

I approached the door to her apartment and waited for her to answer after I knocked. When she finally opened the door, I couldn't help the slow perusal my eyes made over her. Her hair was wrapped up and damned if she didn't look good as hell rocking a bandana. She was wearing loose jogging pants and a white tank, but what was truly stealing all my attention was the imprint of her nipples that were visible through her tank.

"This is a surprise," she said. "Did you need something?"

Shit. I could think of a lot of things that I needed. I also knew that now wasn't the time for what I had in mind. "I was wondering if you needed help with anything today."

She quirked an eyebrow. "Did I miss the memo that you could bake because that's what I'll be doing all day."

I laughed. "I don't bake a whole lot, but I can cook my ass off. If you show me, I'm sure I'll be an asset."

Her mouth twisted as if she were debating between letting me in and telling me to get lost. Any other time, she wouldn't hesitate to send me on my merry way. Which is why I was completely surprised when she stepped back from the door and said, "You can help me. But the minute you get in my way, I'm sending you out of my kitchen and to my damn couch."

I smiled as if my favorite team had won in the playoffs. It was hard to believe that one night had changed our dynamic, but it had. I'd felt it last night and I felt it this morning if the fact that she said she'd punish me to the couch rather than kicking me out was any indication.

Jordyn's place was located on the top floor of her building, so I knew she had the largest home in the building. But this was my first time being in her place.

"Wow," I said as we approached her kitchen. It was huge. Much bigger than that of other apartments this size. She had two ovens, two dishwashers, and two sinks. Her cabinets reached to the ceiling while ample counter space gave her plenty of room to bake. "You must have had this remodeled."

She smiled. "Perks of owning the entire building. I have a large kitchen in my bar as well."

I took a seat on one of her bar stools. "With all this space, you still thought about moving unless you purchased my building?"

She sighed. "I have more apartment buildings here than you do, so I have more tenants. I also had to set aside some storage space for them, and since I have ten employees at the bar, they are always in and out of every place in this building."

"I get it," I said, nodding my head. "Maybe it will help if the main entrance to get into the private room was through my basement instead of yours. I have enough space in my building to cut off my basement and I'm still renovating the space. That way, you could avoid someone accidently discovering it."

She leaned against the counter and studied my eyes. "Last night, I told you a secret about me that not many know, and although in my eyes it's not illegal, in the eyes of the government, it's a different story. Yet, you're willing to let me use your space?"

I shrugged. "Yeah. As long as you let me help."

"I get it," she said with a laugh. "Last night, you weren't just offering to help me fulfill this big order. You want in on my business."

"Yes and no," I said honestly. "I wouldn't want to profit off your empire, but if you decide to use my basement as your main entry, I would hope that you know I'm available to help whenever you need me. Whether that be baking, helping you organize the private room, offering some manpower if you get some deliveries, or move something heavy. Or even keeping an eye out for things if you're out of town. Whatever you need."

The smile that crossed her face was slow and one I hadn't seen before. I typically wasn't the recipient of Jordyn's soft smiles. Mainly because I annoyed her so much, she was fussing with me, not smiling. "Thank you. I'll keep that in mind." She held my gaze for a few more seconds before she glanced down at her counter. "But first, I have to test your baking skills. If you're good, I'll give you an edible."

"And if I'm bad?" I hadn't meant for my voice to drop an octave, but I knew it had affected her when her eyes filled with an interest that hadn't been there before.

"If you suck at baking, I'll still give you an edible. But there's no way I'll let you touch a spatula in my kitchen again."

Jordyn took out a range of ingredients that I was semi-familiar with before pulling out a couple jars of weed. As she gave me a run down on the cupcakes and cookies she was baking for this client, I couldn't help but think about how weird it was for us to be working together like this. It felt comfortable. Natural.

"So, how many co-workers do I have?" I asked when I started prepping the pans as she'd instructed me to do.

She laughed as she continued rolling some cookie dough. "I have ten people in management, including a lawyer and accountant. Fifteen at my warehouse in Maine.

And twenty contract employees that consist of deliverers and ambassadors. Every employee had to go through process training to ensure they could maintain secrecy and represent Heavenly Hash."

"Heavenly Hash? I didn't even think to ask what the name of your business was. Did you name it that because back in the day, they used to call marijuana hash, right?"

"Sure did. And some people still call it that."

"Clever." I watched her mix another batch of cookies, my mouth watering with how good the cookies that she'd just placed in one of her ovens were smelling. "You know, I didn't get to taste any of those treats you brought me last night, right?"

"I know, sorry. I hadn't meant to get a call from my manager about the bar, so I grabbed the tray and rushed to my bar."

"Did everything work out?"

She nodded. "Yeah, my manager was just worried about a woman who seemed a little too intoxicated and a guy that was trying to take her home. We kicked him out, ignoring the curse words he spit our way, and paid a taxi to take her home."

"That was nice of you," I stated. "I would have done the same thing."

She glanced up from what she was doing and caught my eye. "I know you would have."

The way she was looking at me made me feel like she was seeing me in a different light than before. *Either that, or you caught her on a good day.* Only time would tell. I was pretty sure this was the longest we'd gone without fighting.

When she bent over to check on the cookies a few minutes later, I told myself not to look down her shirt. Seconds later, I lost that battle.

"Were you looking down my shirt?" she asked when she stood back up.

"If you didn't want me to look, you shouldn't have bent over for so long."

She rolled her eyes. "I'm baking and I need to make sure my desserts don't burn. If you're going to help me out, you have to keep your hands and eyes to yourself."

I stopped my prep work.

"I thought we had an understanding."

"We do," I replied with a shrug. "But the NDA I signed said nothing about keeping my hands and my eyes to myself. Even if you had put a no-touching clause, I damn sure would never have signed it if it mentioned that I couldn't look at you. I don't know a dude on the planet who would agree to shit like that."

Her face scrunched together the way it did right before she got upset. I would always be respectful, but I'd gone too long without getting a rise from her, so I continued by saying, "If I want to look at that ass, I'll look at that ass. If I want to look at your breasts, I'll look at your breasts. If I want to kiss you senseless like I did on New Year's, I'll do that, too. Point is, I've been doing whatever the fuck I want to do since I hit puberty, so I'll keep your secret, but I can look at whatever I damn well please."

Her breathing grew staggered and the line in her forehead popped. "When hell freezes over," she yelled. And just like that, the Crayson and Jordyn show that our friends loved to watch was back in business.

Jordyn

As crazy as it sounded, I'd really enjoyed baking with Crayson. He hadn't been as bad as I thought he would have been. He knew his way around the kitchen, and after eight hours straight of baking, I was glad that I'd hit my quota for the day, but I was dead tired.

Now, he was in the bathroom cleaning off all of the flour that had gotten on him, giving me a moment to gather my thoughts. *Oh come on, girlfriend. You already know all your thoughts are about him.* As sad as it sounded, when we'd first began baking together, I almost fucked up a batch of cookies when he rolled up the sleeves of his grey sweater to knead some dough and butter some pans.

The way his arm muscles had moved underneath the cotton looked much more erotic than it should considering he was fully clothed. *And don't forget about the peek-a-boo his tats were doing.* One of the things that I always found sexy on Crayson—despite my best efforts to ignore it—was his tattoo sleeve. I was a sucker for a tatted man, and he had an arm full of tattoos just waiting for me to run my fingers over them. Better yet, I wanted to run my tongue over them and follow the black lines to see if they really stopped on his arm, or if they went to other parts of his body.

I sighed, placing the dirty dishes in my dishwasher before wiping down the counters. Before I knew it, my mind was on Crayson again. *Shit.* A bitch could daydream about a man like Crayson all day, which is precisely why I needed to ignore all of the naughty words that seemed to flow from his mouth like a sweet song to Diamond.

Ignore him? For what?!?! You haven't had sex in over eighteen months. I gasped as I swatted my hand in the air like I was swatting away a fly. I never, *ever* talked about how long it had been since I'd had sex, let alone think it. To think it was to accept it, and I refused to accept the fact that it had been too damn long since I'd felt a man's hands on my body.

"Then it's settled," I said aloud. "Ignore. Ignore. Ignore."

"Ignore what?"

Damn. Closing my eyes, I tried to wish him back into the bathroom so I could have a few more moments to think clearly. I didn't want to look in the direction of Crayson's voice. Not until I was confident my face didn't give away what I really wanted.

"Are you okay?" he asked, coming up from behind me.

"Yeah, I'm fine."

"Are you sure?" I could feel his warm breath on the side of my neck, so I knew he was close. "Because you were talking to yourself. Anything I can help you with?"

You can help me by turning me around and lifting me onto my countertop before you fuck me until the sun comes up. "Nope. All good here."

He didn't say anything for a while, and I could still feel him standing behind me. "Do you want to watch a movie?" I asked as I got back to washing the counters. *Watch a movie? Really, Jordyn?* I should have been thanking him for helping me bake and making up a lie about being tired or something. Instead, my excuse to give myself more space was to ask him to stay longer? Something was seriously fucked up with the way my brain was working.

"A movie sounds good," he said. "I saw some popcorn in one of your cabinets. Care if I make a bag?"

"Nope." I threw the dishrag in the sink. "In fact, you do that and I'll pick out a movie." I wanted to run to the living room, but I walked as normally as I could. By the time I'd turned on my television and gone to my Netflix app, I'd already scrolled through several romantic comedies and settled on an action flick when Crayson walked into the living room holding a bowl of popcorn and two water bottles.

"Good choice," he said, placing everything on my coffee table before sitting next to me on my couch. "I love any shit that Samuel L. Jackson is in."

"Me too." I opened my water bottle to take a sip when I remembered something important. I went to the kitchen and returned with one of the cupcakes I'd baked. "I almost forgot that you have to try this."

He smiled. "Does that mean I passed the baking test?"

I shrugged. "You were okay."

He shook his head before he took a bite into the cupcake. I hadn't even noticed that I was holding my breath, awaiting his reaction, until his eyes widened in pleasure.

"Holy shit. This cupcake is good as hell." He took two more bites. "I can taste a hint of weed, but I barely taste it. I've had some bad edibles, but this is blended to perfection."

"Thank you. I worked hard to concoct the perfect amount of ingredients."

"Well you achieved it." He tossed the rest of the cupcake into his mouth before taking a drink of water.

As the movie began, I got annoyed with myself by how much his opinion meant to me. I prided myself on never caring what others thought about what I did or what I created as long as I'm confident in what I'm doing. Yet, here I was, hanging on Crayson's every word.

Just try and watch the movie. I tried my best to get comfortable and stay on my side of the couch, but it wasn't working. I rearranged myself several times before settling on tucking my right foot under my left leg, and even then, I was still fidgety.

Damn, bitch. Sit still! I wasn't even an antsy person, but being this close to Crayson was fucking with my nerves. As rude as it sounded, I felt like I needed to kick him out of my place if I was going to relax at all before spending all day at the bar tomorrow.

"You worry too damn much."

I turned to Crayson, his voice cutting through my thoughts. "You talking to me?"

"I don't see any other woman in here trippin' since she's had me in her place all day." He looked my way and met my eyes. "What the hell are you thinking so hard about?"

I frowned. "Not that I have to explain myself to you, but I was watching the movie."

"Not really," he said. "You were looking at the TV, but your mind was on me. You may be telling yourself that you were trying to figure out a way to kick my ass out, but deep down, you really want me to stay. So quick overthinking this shit and enjoy the damn movie. And sit still, too. Every time you fidget, it distracts me from the movie."

"Oh hell no." I scooted closer to him. "Who do you think you're talking to? No man tells me what to do and when to do it, asshole."

A sly smile filled his face. "JayJay, I may be an asshole, but you'd eat a polite man alive."

"You must have lost your goddamn mind using my nickname *again* after I told you not to use it." I got even more into his face, my temper slowly rising.

"That may be the case," he said, "but I've learned something about you."

"And what's that?" My voice still dripped with attitude, but I didn't care. He'd pissed me off.

His eyes softened. "Jordyn, I just want to sit here and enjoy this movie with you. Maybe even convince you to lean into me so we can watch it more comfortably." He briefly looked to my lips. "I won't act like I don't want to kiss that attitude off your lips right now, but I'm learning that you're more comfortable when you're arguing with me about something than you are when we're getting along. I only pissed you off just now so that you could try and focus on that, and not whatever else was going on in that beautiful head of yours."

Wow. I opened my mouth to respond, but no words came out. I felt like it was the type of moment when I really needed to put my words together, but after a few awkward seconds, Crayson pulled me to him so that I was positioned in the crook of his arm.

"Relax," he whispered. "I heard this is a great movie."

I didn't dare look up at him, so instead, I took his advice and tried my best to relax. By the time we'd reached the middle of the movie, the popcorn and water were gone, and I was still in the same spot I was when he'd pulled me to him. It was the most relaxed I'd been in years.

NINE

Crayson

"Damn. I hope this wraps up soon." I glanced at my copper watch before turning to Malakai. "Please tell me this is the last location on the list."

"I wish," Malakai huffed. "When Avery first told me that we'd be tasting different wedding cakes today, it sounded fun. Taste some cake. Sip some champagne. But this shit is on a whole other level. She's usually not even the type to want to stunt on other females, but with this cake she's all 'wedding cakes get a bad rep, so ours has to taste the best and have the perfect mix of flavors.' And the worst part is, bro, I can't even tell her that's she's taking this shit too seriously because I'm not trying to piss her off."

I shook my head with a laugh. "This is why I'm never getting married. Females always think they can change you, and if they can't, you spend the rest of the relationship trying to hide who you really are just so they can think you're a changed man."

Malakai laughed. "Your views are truly fucked up sometimes."

"Are you saying I'm wrong?"

"Yeah, bruh, that's exactly what I'm saying." He waved his hand in Avery's direction. "That woman over there may drive me crazy sometimes, but being with her made me want to be a better man. I'm not saying I wasn't a good man before she met me because if I hadn't been, she wouldn't have given me the time of day. But the right woman can change a man in ways he never saw coming. I fight harder, I push harder, because now, building a great life ain't just for me, it's for us and our future kids. So yeah, you're wrong, but you'll get me when you find a woman who's willing to put up with your bullshit."

I grunted. "Women just make things complicated. Just take me and Jordyn for example. We aren't even dating. We're barely friends. Yet, I already have to change the way I act around her if I want to have a peaceful conversation without her cursing me out."

I felt someone push me on my shoulder and turned to see Jordyn roll her eyes. "Or stop saying dumb shit and I won't have to curse you out."

I rubbed the spot she hit even though it didn't really hurt. "You'd curse me out regardless." I glanced around and found a couple chairs at the front of the bakery. "Man, I'll be sitting in one of those chairs until the ladies narrow down the flavors we need to taste," I whispered to Malakai.

He bumped my fist. "Bet. Wish I could join you."

I settled into the uncomfortable wicker chair and closed my eyes. Typically, I was amped at the start of the weekend, but today, that wasn't the case. It was Friday afternoon and

I'd spent the entire morning training the supervisor and manager of my Brooklyn cigar lounge, Undefined Sanctum. It still wasn't ready for the engagement party or grand opening yet, but I wanted them to get a feel for the layout before everything was complete.

They both had given me some great feedback, and since my contractor was there as well, we'd tweaked the floorplan to avoid any future issues. I'd been so busy, that I hadn't even seen Jordyn all week.

Spending most of the weekend with her had been better than I ever thought it would have. We still bickered over some shit, but even the disagreements seemed to be laced with something that I couldn't understand. I'd sensed that telling me about Heavenly Hash had lifted a burden since she'd really had her eyes set on making that private room operational for her business.

I didn't want my contractor and his team anywhere near the basement, so I was going to take that project on by myself. Jordyn hadn't liked the idea of me working for free and she knew damn well I wouldn't accept her money. So she offered to work with me, and I hadn't even tried to hide my excitement. I was growing on her whether she wanted to admit it or not.

In my fucking world, we would have been able to spend the afternoon developing a plan for demo'ing the space and getting it ready for her supplies, but instead, we were both being dragged around New York City on a wild goose chase for wedding cake. Jordyn seemed to be enjoying the shit. I, on the other hand, could think of a hundred things I'd rather be doing.

I'd barely been sitting for five minutes before Malakai told me that we were moving to a private room for the tasting.

"Bruh, why the hell do they need us here for this shit?" Avery and Jordyn were chatting with the fourth baker of the day. Had I known choosing the perfect cake would take five hours, I would have brought my ass home.

"Okay," the baker said, clasping her hands together. "Now that we're all seated, we can start." Her assistant placed trays filled with an assortment of cake flavors in front of each of us. "We're going to start the tasting from left to right. On your trays, you have the following flavors: red velvet, yellow, chocolate, carrot, coconut, lemon berry, chocolate raspberry, salted caramel, cookies and cream, fresh strawberries and cream, southern hazelnut, and one of my personal favorites, dark chocolate ganache."

"Damn, this is the narrowed down version," I said aloud before I could stop myself. I was met with three sets of piercing eyes. Surprisingly, Jordyn was the first one to drop the death stare.

"If you want to keep all your fingers, you better get with the program," Jordyn whispered. "Avery has a small case of bridezilla syndrome."

I nodded my head and continued the tasting on my best behavior, until we tasted the chocolate raspberry. I hadn't even been able to swallow that poor excuse for a cake flavor. I didn't care if it was one of the most popular flavors like the baker said. It tasted like shit, and although I may talk a lot of shit, I didn't want to eat it.

"Hell nah." I spit that crap out in my napkin. When I looked back to the baker she wasn't happy.

"Can we move on?" the baker asked me.

Can we not? "Yeah, go ahead." For the rest of the tasting, I took much smaller bites.

TEN

Crayson

AT THE END OF THE TASTING, AVERY AND MALAKAI had settled on the dark chocolate ganache and had decided to treat Jordyn and I to dinner at a nearby jazz lounge. By the time we finished dinner, the lounge and dance floor were packed. Malakai pulled Avery to the dance floor, leaving Jordyn and I alone in the booth.

Our waiter refilled our drinks and gave us the tip that we may want to hold onto our table if we planned on staying longer. So we settled into the seats.

"Are you glad cake tasting is over?" she asked, taking a sip of her red wine.

"Hell yeah. I like cake, but we were doing too damn much today."

She giggled. "I agree. I had to be a good maid of honor, so I tried to fake it, but I didn't like most of that cake we tried today."

"Why didn't you offer to make their wedding cake? Your desserts taste way better than that mess we had today."

She smiled. "I did offer, but Avery felt like she was giving me enough duties to do. Plus, she wants some elaborate design and I'm more of a cupcake kind of girl. I can bake cakes, but I'd rather not. I think she knows that about me."

"Makes sense," I said, nodding my head. "But had they picked chocolate raspberry as their flavor, I would have thrown yo' ass to the wolves and told them you were making the damn cake, or I wasn't coming to the wedding."

"You're so dramatic," she said with a laugh. "Real talk though, that flavor tasted like shit."

My eyes widened. "That's exactly what I thought. I spit it out because I refused to swallow it. I still have an aftertaste from it."

"Me too," she agreed. "A part of me wondered if they'd baked it with actual *shit*."

We both started laughing before settling into a comfortable silence, the music around us soothing, yet popping at the same time. "I wish I enjoyed jazz more."

"Me too," Jordyn said with a yawn. "Don't get me wrong, I like jazz. But I'm not the type to listen to it for more than a couple songs. I much more prefer R&B or hip hop, but if given the choice, I'd choose hip hop all of the time."

I tilted my mouth in surprise. "I didn't peg you for a hip hop kind of woman."

She glanced around before scooting closer to me in the booth and said, "You also didn't peg me for a Marijuana Queenpin. Yet, here I am. Wowing you and shit."

"So you do like the nickname," I said with a laugh. "When we're around our friends, I'll just call you MQ."

Her eyes widened. "I don't like it that damn much, but I like it a helluva lot better than this jazz music right now." She glanced around again. "Want to try a new dessert I made this morning?"

I quirked an eyebrow, hoping it was laced with a certain something to help us get through this night. "An edible?"

She nodded her head and pulled out a colorful concoction. "I made colorful rice crispy treat bites and brought a couple with me in case you were up for trying it."

I smiled, touched that she'd been thinking about me. I popped the small treat into my mouth, waiting for the taste of weed to hit, but instantly met with some sugary flavors instead. "Holy shit. This packs some flavor."

"That's the idea," she said with a smile before popping one into her mouth. "The small treats I make are great for relaxation or meditation. This rice crispy treat is a new one for me, so I'm hoping my bigger clients enjoy the samples I'm sending out tomorrow."

While Jordyn explained a little more about some additional desserts that were in the works, it hit me that I could listen to her talk about this for hours, which was crazy because I'd never been the type to listen to anyone talk for hours.

After a while, we settled into our seats, the effects of the rice crispy treat already working its relaxation magic. My eyes went back to the dance floor. I immediately smiled when my brother dipped Avery to the sound of the saxophone. "Malakai and Avery are loving this shit."

"I know." Jordyn turned to watch them dance. "They are too cute. I am so happy they found each other."

I smiled. "Me too. My brother didn't have it easy with relationships in the past, so I'm glad he found Avery."

Jordyn turned back to face me. "What about you? Have

you had it easy in relationships or more of a rocky road? No, wait." She put a hand up to stop me from responding. "Let me guess. Infamous fuckboy Crayson Madden doesn't do relationships, so the answer is yes, you've had it easy as hell."

"I'm offended." I placed my hands over my chest. "Who said I was a fuckboy? I've got standards."

She raised an eyebrow. "I didn't say you didn't have standards, but you know you're a fuckboy so that's not up for discussion. I'm sure I could back up my claim and find twenty women you've slept with in Brooklyn alone since you've purchased your location."

I took a sip of my Cognac, wondering if she knew how wrong she was. I hadn't even fucked a woman since I'd kissed Jordyn on New Year's, but she didn't need to know that. She was already fucking with my state of mind enough.

Just a few weeks ago, I'd gone on a date with one of my regulars. After the date, I'd taken her to her home with every intention of sleeping with her and picking up where we left off a couple months ago. Yet, once I'd walked into her place, I made up some lame ass excuse and left.

On my drive back home, I'd almost crashed when I realized that I'd turned down some good pussy for some pussy I may never get. Jordyn had me by the dick, and right now, she didn't know the power she had over me. It was in my best interest to keep it that way.

"I didn't have it easy," I said, finally answering her question. She studied my eyes, waiting for me to explain more, but I wasn't sure I could. I'd never talked to anyone about my ex, Danielle. The only one who knew anything about her was Malakai, and at the time he'd been going through his own shit, so I'd dealt with working through my anger myself.

You want to tell her. You want Jordyn to know. I ran my fingers down my face, not believing that I wanted to tell her some shit I'd buried deep in my mind and left for dead. However, that's exactly what happened when I told her, "Most people think I run through multiple women without giving any fucks about how it looks to others, but having that persona was never my intention. Yeah, I enjoy fucking women, but they know the deal when they lay in bed with me. I have a few on rotation, but that's it."

Her fingers played with the rim of her glass. "You say that like having a rotation of women that you sleep with is the most normal thing in the world."

"It is," I said. "Better than sleeping with twenty women a month like folks think I do. My starting lineup is less than five, and those chicks know if they even try to tie me down, I'm eliminating them from my roster."

Her robust laugh caught me off guard. "Oh my God, you truly are an asshole. Eliminated from your roster? Who are you to dictate if a woman catches feelings or not? I know yo' dick ain't that good."

Now it was my turn to laugh. "I keep tryin' to show you my moves on the court, but you steady turning me down. If you'd dribble the ball, maybe you'd score."

"Enough with the cheesy basketball references." I heard what she was saying, but I also knew she was holding in her laugh. She liked my cheesy references whether she admitted it or not. "All I'm saying is a man who sleeps around with every female they meet is bound to have an easier time in relationships than someone like Malakai who wanted to find that special love. In the end, what you're doing with these women is a relationship whether you see it that way or not. It may be a fuck buddies type of thing. But you're getting all of the perks a boyfriend gets without having to put in the work." She adjusted herself in her seat. "Like I said. Easy."

I shook my head. "I see how you would think that, but to me, those aren't relationships at all. With every woman I sleep with, my heart is cut off from it. I only had to make that mistake one time for me to see that relationships weren't for me."

She squinted her eyes as she took another sip of her wine. "What happened? Did an ex-girlfriend cheat on you?"

"Something like that." I finished off my glass of Cognac and met her inquisitive eyes. She wanted to know why I was the way I was and I wanted to tell her. So I did. "I wish like hell she'd cheated on me when she was still my girlfriend. But nah, she had to disrespect my ass after I'd made her my wife."

Jordyn slammed her wine glass down on the table and started coughing, clearly caught off guard by what I'd said. Although there was nothing funny about what I'd revealed, I almost wanted to laugh. She thought she had me pegged as the playa type, and although I wasn't denying that I was now, it hadn't always been the case. At least not with my ex. I'd sworn before God and Malakai as our witness that she would never want for anything.

She'd had my nose wide the fuck open and had I been more careful, I would have seen that she was trash. I would have noticed that she'd never really loved me the way I'd loved her. She was a liar. A cheater. I should have watched my back. *But you hadn't because you cared about her so much.* Better yet, I'd been too in love to see what was right in front of my face.

Looking at the woman sitting across from me, I had to remind myself not to repeat that shit.

Jordyn

WHAT. THE. FUCK. I WANTED TO RESPOND TO WHAT he'd just said, but I was too busy coughing my lungs up. "You can't say such surprising shit when someone is taking a sip of something," I rasped in between breaths.

"Sorry," he said with a laugh. "That wasn't my intention."

Once I had my coughing under control, I finally asked him why I never knew he'd been married before.

He briefly glanced to the dance floor. "None of our friends know. Only Malakai. My ex, Danielle, and I had eloped, so I didn't even tell my parents or my brothers."

"Why not tell your family?" He was close to his family, so that surprised me. I watched him clench and unclench his jaw.

"Did you meet my brothers and parents the night Malakai proposed to Avery?"

I nodded my head. "Briefly, but I met them."

"Then you know how well-liked they all are." He waved the waiter over and ordered another drink before continuing. "My parents are like the mom and dad of the entire community back in our Arkansas hometown. Caden is the typical all-American cowboy next door. Malik and Malakai are loved by everyone. Even Micah, who's gotten in his fair share of trouble, is usually accepted and welcomed wherever he goes. And folks haven't even seen Carter in years since he's in the military, yet, they still stop by my parents B&B asking how he's doing and saying how great it is that he's serving his country. Not to mention, everyone in my family is successful."

There was something in the way he'd said the statement that made me feel like he was excluding himself from that last part. Therefore, I only felt it was right to remind him, "So are you. You own three cigar lounges in New York. That's pretty damn successful."

"Thank you. I am successful, but I'm also the one people always assume will fuck up. Don't get me wrong, I know it's valid since I've done my share of fucked up shit and my bluntness rubs a lot of folks the wrong way, but that's not my badge of dishonor. That's not what I want to be known as."

"You think your family would have considered your marriage a fuck up?" I asked. "Is that why you didn't tell them?"

"I didn't think they would, I knew they would. You see, growing up, I didn't hang out with the best crowd. I was always doing some shit I shouldn't be doing. I may not have been the one breaking into buildings and stealing shit, but I hung out with the guys who did so I was there for it all. Back then, I thought I owed these guys everything. Hell, I even learned how to drive in the cars they'd stolen."

"I get it," I said. "You were guilty by association."

"Pretty much. And if one of us got caught doing reckless shit, the guys knew I wouldn't talk if I was the one to get caught. But that shit got old real quick, and after a few run ins with the cops and a heart-to-heart with my dad, I got my GED, then decided to move out here to New York since Malakai was already out here."

"And you are the closest to Malakai out of all of your brothers, right?"

He smiled in a way that made me smile. "Yeah, we've always been tight. Malakai always understood me, and while I was getting on my brothers' and my parents' nerves, he took the time to build a close relationship with me. No one was surprised when I followed him to New York. But he wasn't about to let my ass get wrapped up in the same shit I was back in Arkansas.

"College wasn't for me, so I was working odd end jobs when I'd moved out here. I'd been working as a personal trainer at the gym when I'd met Danielle. Remember when I mentioned that I knew Stephen, Mr. Briggs' son?"

I nodded my head. "Yes, I remember."

"I used to train him, so after his personal training session, we'd often hit up this restaurant were Danielle worked. She had a friend who worked there too named Sara. Stephen had been really into Sara and I was into Danielle, so naturally, the four of us started hanging out. For the first couple years of our relationship, things were great."

"Until they weren't," I said, reflecting on my own failed relationship.

"Exactly." He took another sip of his drink. "Things progressed pretty quickly and I introduced her to Malakai. They got along pretty well, and once Stephen and Sara married and moved out of state, we got even closer."

"Did she ever meet your other brothers and your parents?"

"Nah, I never introduced them. Neither one of our families were from New York, so it was easy to keep our family life separate from our relationship. I didn't realize at the time, I'd at least told her all about my family and introduced her to one of my brothers, but I didn't know anything about her. After dating for a year, we eloped in Vegas with Malakai as our witness. That's when everything went to shit.

"I was the best personal trainer at the gym, but I knew I wanted to do something else, I just didn't know what. Danielle had bigger dreams, too. She'd only had a year left of credits to finish at a local college before she could get her degree, so I got another part-time job at a cigar store to help pay for her education. Working at the cigar store, everything clicked for me. Suddenly, I knew what I wanted to do, but when I told Danielle, she hadn't been supportive. She wanted even more and started telling me that my lack of college education was bothering her. She felt like opening a cigar lounge would cost unnecessary money and would fail within the first year."

"That's ridiculous," I said. "You supported her dreams, so the least she could have done was support yours."

"Malakai said the same thing back then. So did Stephen when I'd called and asked his advice. Little had I known, nothing would have saved my marriage. Danielle had already been sleeping with this lawyer behind my back. When I caught them together in our bed, I'd been out for blood. He better thank his lucky stars that Malakai had been with me, because I wanted to kill him. Instead of feeling remorse, Danielle told me that I'd never be the type of man he was and she wanted a divorce."

"That's bullshit," I said, shaking my head. "You gave her everything and she responded by cheating on you."

Crayson nodded his head. "Turns out, they'd been sleeping together since the week after we got married. Yet, Danielle got hers because she thought he wanted to be with her, but he didn't. The day our divorce was final, he broke up with her, so she was left without a house and a way to pay for her education."

"Please tell me you didn't help her out."

"I didn't, but that day will be one I'll always regret. Not because I wish we would have worked it out, but because I'd been a dumb ass and had given her the courtesy of packing up the rest of her shit without me there. I didn't believe in banks back then and I'd never told her where I'd kept my stash of money that I was saving to purchase my first storefront. But she found it anyway, and when I returned later that night, Danielle and all my money was gone."

My eyes widened. "Did you ever get your money back?"

"Nah, I didn't. I didn't report it either. I was ready to be done with her. At first, I couldn't believe that she'd done that to me, but then I thought long and hard about the situation and realized that our relationship had been over way before she'd agreed to marry me. I'd hung on to the hope that she'd loved me as much as I'd loved her. I'd thought when we'd made that commitment, she'd meant it as much as I did. I wanted to be the man she told me she dreamed of when she was a little girl. I wanted to be her *everything*. Yet, she just wanted a money ticket out of the restaurant where she worked."

I studied his eyes, seeing a vulnerability I'd never noticed before. *Damn.* She'd really done a number on him, but I understood the feeling all too well. "I'm sorry you went through that. I've been where you are, and being cheated on by someone you trust is the worst feeling in the world."

He studied my eyes while I told him, " I hope you realize that your past doesn't define you. Take it from someone who knows this all too well." One would think that

Heavenly Hash was my biggest secret, but it wasn't. Not by a long shot.

"I feel you, but as much as I wished it hadn't impacted me, it did. The day my divorce was finalized was the day I stopped giving a shit about love."

I took a sip of water, ignoring the fact that his words disappointed me. He didn't owe me a damn thing, and what he'd said shouldn't have affected me, but it did.

I hated to sound hopeful when Crayson wasn't my man and probably never would be. *And you don't want him to be, girl. Get a grip!* However, that didn't stop me from asking, "Do you ever think you will give it another try?"

I hoped my voice gave away the fact that I really wanted to know his answer. I felt like I was holding my breath for his response until he finally said, "My first instinct was to say *hell nah.*" He held my gaze and the intense look in his eyes made me want to melt into my seat. "Now, I'm not so sure."

It was at the tip of my tongue to ask why he wasn't sure now of all times, but I didn't. Truth was, I wasn't sure I was prepared to handle his answer. Especially since I was seeing Crayson through a new pair of eyes.

We'd never gotten along long enough to have an actual conversation that was uninterrupted by bickering. Now that we had, I didn't want to admit how much I liked it ... How deep down, I hoped that I was the reason he thought about giving love a second shot.

ELEVEN

Crayson

THE PAST FEW DAYS HAD BEEN BUSIER THAN I WOULD have liked, but I was glad that all of the major work for Undefined Sanctum was almost complete. *Just in time for Malakai and Avery's engagement party this weekend.*

Yesterday, I'd finally gotten a chance to start working on carving out a doorway for the entrance from my basement to the private room between my building and Jordyn's. I'd only seen Jordyn in passing since I'd shared my story about my ex the other night, so I was excited to give her an update on the private room.

We'd agreed to meet up tonight to discuss the engagement party and I was looking forward to seeing her fine ass again. It wasn't every day that I opened up like I had to her, but she'd listened and understood me. I wanted to know more about her, too. I wanted to know what had happened with her ex to make her relate to me on another level, but I had to be patient with Jordyn. It wasn't long ago that she couldn't stand my ass.

"Wat up, Greg," I said, greeting one of the bartenders as I walked into Sweet Baby Jay's. "Is Jordyn around?"

"What's good, fam." He nodded to right. "She's in her office. She's expecting you, so you can head on back."

I walked down the long, narrow hallway, surveying my surroundings since this was the first time I'd ever been back here. As I got closer to the only open door at the end of the hallway, I overheard her talking on the phone.

"Grandpa, I understand how you and the family feel, but I'm not sure I'm ready yet." Her voice sounded strained, and even though I couldn't hear the person on the other end, I figured she was trying to explain herself based off what I could hear. When I reached her office entranceway, her back was turned toward me as she looked up to the ceiling.

"I know, I know. I agree, it's been too long. Tell you what, can I think about it?" She sighed, apparently not liking the response. "No one understands but me. You all may think you do, but you have no idea the pain I feel daily. The suffering I go through daily. It's ... It's unbearable sometimes."

The pain she feels? Damn. I'd never heard Jordyn talk like that before. Although I'd like to think that I'd cared about a woman since my catastrophe of a marriage to Danielle, listening to Jordyn speak, I knew that wasn't the case. Her words hit me square in the gut and in ways I'd never expected. The pain in her voice stroked my skin in an unwanted touch. She sounded defeated. Overwhelmed even.

Standing there, seeing her stiff posture and the way her free hand rubbed the back of her neck, I realized that I didn't know much about her family. Since Avery was engaged to Malakai, Jordyn knew much more about my family than vice versa. As a matter of fact, the only shit I'd learned was what she'd told me a few weeks ago. Had she not needed my cooperation with the private room, I probably wouldn't know a damn thing about her.

Jordyn was a private person and I respected that shit because in some ways, I was private, too. Folks only saw the part of me that could be loud and somewhat obnoxious at times. Yet, they rarely took the time to see the man behind the bluntness. Jordyn always had her shit together and seldom did you see her falter in her confident steps. But tonight, she wasn't the Jordyn everybody often saw.

Not wanting to eavesdrop anymore without her knowing, I lightly knocked on the open door. Sad eyes met mine as she motioned for me to take a seat on the couch. Although she may not have felt her best, she damn sure looked it. She was wearing a tight black top that was tucked into the jeans hugging her apple bottom ass. Her short, curly hair always looked good, but tonight, the slightly untamed look made her facial features appear softer for some reason.

A couple minutes later, she wrapped up her conversation and gathered her notepad and pen before telling me, "I'm sorry about that. I love him like crazy, but my grandpa doesn't understand the meaning of a quick call."

"No worries." She sat next to me on the couch, giving me a better look at her. Worry lines I hadn't been able to see before were evident in her forehead and the corners of her eyes.

"Since we already sent out the invitations for the party, I figured we could start on the order of events," she said. "We're celebrating Avery and Malakai, so that's the main focus." As she continued telling me her ideas, it was obvious that her mind was somewhere else.

I stopped her pen from jotting down notes before asking her, "Are you okay? You don't seem like yourself."

I expected her to say she was fine, hoping I'd let it go. However, she did the complete opposite when she told me, "No, I'm not okay."

"What can I do to help?" Taking her notepad and pen out of her hands, I placed them back on her desk.

"I-I can't ... I can't b-believe ..." she stammered as she tried to gather her words. "Never mind. I'm usually better at hiding my emotions. Just forget I said anything. It'll be fine."

"What will be fine?" I asked.

She shook her head. "I meant, I would be fine. Not it. Nothing's wrong, I'm just stressed about meeting the Heavenly Hash deadline since it's crunch time. Plus, there's some stuff going on with the bar."

I didn't believe her, but I didn't want to push her too much. Instead of questioning her further, I pulled her closer to me. For an instant, she was stiff in my arms, but slowly, she began to relax as she placed her head on my chest.

"Whatever it is, it will be okay," I reassured.

"I hope so," she murmured. "I just wish I could clear my mind and forget about everything going on."

My fingers ran up and down her back in calming strokes as I let her words sink in. There was nothing more I wanted to do than to help her forget about the shit she had on her mind. But I had to tread lightly.

I slightly lifted her from my chest so that I could look her dead in her eyes when I asked, "On a scale of one to ten, how badly do you want to lose yourself right now?"

Her eyes searched mine, as if trying to pinpoint what my angle was. If she said anything that wasn't a ten, I'd drop the question. However, if she said the number I hoped she said, I wasn't backing down.

"A ten," she whispered. "On a scale of one to ten, I want to fully lose myself right now." Her voice was stronger when she'd said the last part, giving me the confirmation that I'd been waiting for. Just as quickly as she'd voiced the words, her eyes began to fill with a slight panic.

"Don't worry," I assured. "We won't be having sex tonight if that's what you were wondering." I may be an asshole, but I wasn't a user and there was no way in hell I was taking advantage of Jordyn right now. I needed to know what was wrong with her before my dick felt what it was like to be inside of her, but that didn't mean I couldn't make her lose herself in the meantime.

She glanced away, but not before I saw the flicker of disappointment cross her face.

"I have a question for your, Jordyn." Placing my hand under her chin, I lifted her head so that her almond-shaped eyes were locked onto mine. "I won't fuck you when your head may not be in it, but I can give you a release. So my question is, how do you want to come?"

Her eyes widened. "What do you mean?"

"You know what I mean." I leaned closer to her left ear to make sure she heard me when I repeated, "I know the look of a woman in need of an orgasm, and I want to be the mutha fucka who gives it to you. So I gotta know ... How do you want to come? On my face, on my hands, or both?"

Her posture straightened, and for a second, I thought I'd gone too far. That maybe she'd changed her mind about wanting to lose herself. But then, her lips slightly parted, her eyelids lowered with desire, and the way she worried her bottom lip gave me all types of dirty ideas. She may not have expected my offer, but she was damn sure contemplating it.

Jordyn

HOW DO YOU WANT TO COME? IF I'D EVER MADE A LIST of the top three things a sexy man could say to make me soak my panties on the spot, Crayson's naughty offer would have been at the top of that list.

Damn, I needed to forget. I needed to lose myself. There was so much going on in my life right now that I thought I was prepared for, but wasn't. Still, I wasn't sure allowing Crayson to go down on me was the answer. Oh, I wanted it. Badly. But, how could I let him do that and not give him anything in return?

"I can't," I said, shaking my head. "I would be using your body for my own personal needs."

"Technically, you'd be using my tongue," he said with a shrug.

"Even so, there's no way I can ask you to do that." *Bitch, why the hell not? You need this shit.*

"Shut up, Diamond," I whispered.

He lifted an eyebrow. "What was that?"

"Nothing." I shook my head. "Like I said, I should have never asked you to do something like that."

He pinned me with a lust-filled look that almost made me pant like a damn poodle. "You didn't ask me to do anything. I offered to taste that sweet pussy of yours." His eyes briefly dropped to my lips. "You must know by now that I've been trying to fuck you with my mouth months."

"I thought you were trying to fuck me the good ole' fashioned way."

His mouth curled to the side in a smirk. "Jordyn, I've been trying to fuck you any way you'd let me. Doing so, whether that be with my mouth or my dick, would be an honor. So, if any of your thoughts are ones of doubt that I wouldn't enjoy licking your pussy as much as you'd enjoy riding my tongue, push that shit out of your mind."

Holy shit. Why did everything he say sound so damn dirty? "Okay," I replied in a breathless sigh. "I will."

"Good." He dropped his smirk. "Jordyn, I'll ask you again," he rasped, his voice animal-like in a way that made me shiver in anticipation. "do you want to come on my face, my hands, or both?"

Diamond quivered at the thought, so I told her ass to calm the fuck down since his tongue wasn't even caressing her yet. *In the meantime, you need to calm down, too, Jordyn.* I'd never been a shy person, but Crayson made me nervous in that he-looks-at-me-like-he-wants-to-eat-me-alive kind of way. And damned if I wasn't ready to be devoured.

"Your face," I said confidently. "And then maybe your hands. I guess, I'd rather come on your face, but have your hands help me get there." *Shit, that answer was way too honest.* Then again, from what she knew about Crayson, he appreciated honesty.

"Okay then." And just like that, his lust-filled gaze turned into one that was filled with desire laced with a kind of danger that was all Crayson. He stood to close the door, ck clicking into place signifying that he

hed me again, he motioned for me to is hands going directly to the buckle and jeans while he placed a soft kiss on my lips. His lips left mine as he bent down to help me shimmy out of my pants, removing my boots in the process.

I silently thanked Diamond for telling me that she wanted to wear black lace today because the way Crayson's hands slowly moved up my legs, to my thighs, before cupping my ass, let me know he was enjoying the view.

For a man who always seemed to have something to say, he wasn't doing much talking. It was unnerving in the best way. Turning me around, he softly bit my ass before dragging my panties down my thighs. I could feel everything. Every touch. Every caress. The callouses on his hands. His warm breath as he placed kisses across the backs of my thighs.

"Don't think," he growled. "Just feel." Oh, he didn't have to worry about that at all. There was no way I could do anything other than feel everything he was doing to me.

Once he'd completely removed my panties, he twisted me back around and licked his lips as he stared at my pussy. "More beautiful than I could have imagined." His words sent a shiver running down my spine, but I managed to stay standing. He tapped my thighs for me to widen my legs, rolling his thumb over my clit and causing another shiver to take over my body. *Fuck.* It felt too damn good and it had been way too long since I'd felt something like this.

Slowly, he inserted his middle finger, the angle causing me to buck in place. His finger worked every angle before he added another finger, making me even wetter. Right when I was on the brink of an orgasm, he moved his fingers and leaned back on the couch.

"I don't want you coming like that," he said. "I want you coming on my face."

Lord, give me strength. I couldn't ever recall a man actually telling me that he'd rather I come on his face, than his hands. Then again, Crayson Madden wasn't an ordinary man. Not by a long shot. *This is why he has females out here wildin' out.*

"Um, are you sure?" I always kept Diamond nice and trimmed, but I wasn't sure if Crayson was one of those bare-only types of men.

Instead of responding to me, he pulled me to him, lifting my left leg until I was straddling him. *Oh, shit.* He was hard as hell and his dick was pressing through his jeans and teasing my pussy with all of the possibilities it was capable of. Unable to help myself, I rolled my hips over his dick, enjoying the sensations I felt even though we weren't skin to skin.

He must have read my thoughts because he told me, "Not tonight," before placing his arms under my thighs and pulling me up to his face. Instantly, I felt his warm breath play with my curls, but Crayson didn't even give me a chance to get my bearings. He dipped his tongue inside of my pussy before stroking my clit in a way that had me ready to hop off the damn couch. But I wasn't going anywhere. He had my thighs locked on his face.

"Oh fuck," I moaned, throwing my head to the ceiling and covering my mouth as an onslaught of pleasure ricocheted through my insides. It didn't make no damn sense for me to be hollering like I was, yet, I was sure that every bitch who'd fucked with Crayson understood how I felt. He may be a cocky son-of-a-bitch, but Crayson was an animal with his tongue. Straight beast mode with it.

I went to cover my mouth again, but his hands left my thighs and grabbed my arms. "I don't give a shit if the whole damn bar can hear you moaning as I devour your pussy. The main mutha fucka who wants to hear your moans of satisfaction is me. So, don't cover that beautiful mouth of yours. I want to hear it."

I nodded my head, unable to speak since he was still so close to my pussy, that his words felt like he was caressing my soul. A couple minutes later, my orgasm reached its brink.

"Cray, I'm coming." A bitch couldn't even get out his full name, I was so consumed with pleasure. I tried to glance down at Crayson to see if he'd heard me, but it was no use. He didn't seem to be letting up, and seconds later, my entire body convulsed in an orgasm that rocked me to my core. Crayson didn't let my thighs go, and when the convulsions subsided, his tongue circled my clit in soothing strokes.

When my breathing finally started to go back to normal, Crayson continued to place soft kisses over my pussy, occasionally dipping his tongue into my center. *There's no way,* I thought. *There's no way I can come again so soon.* No sooner than the thought had left my mind did I feel the strokes of his tongue get bolder. Wetter. Not before long, my hips began moving while I rode his tongue for a second time. This time, I said to hell with hiding my moans and I let that shit go.

TWELVE

Jordyn

"Okay, Jordyn, you can do this." I gave myself a pep talk as I walked up to the building that matched the address Avery had texted me. I'd been trying to figure out what I would say to Crayson for the past couple hours since an impromptu visit this early in the morning would definitely need to be explained.

And what if he has another chick here? What if they had sex last night and she's still there? Do I just pretend I didn't really want anything?

"Be chill," I said aloud, halting the direction of my thoughts. "You're just here to say thank you. That's it." I snorted as soon as the comment left my mouth. Two days ago, Crayson had given me not one, but two mind-blowing orgasms, and although he'd seemed content with leaving things as they were, I wasn't. I was horny as hell despite the fact that

Crayson's dick was the last dick on Earth I should be craving. *Girl, please. Your ex, Luther, is the last dick you should want. On the other hand, Crayson's dick had almost made you come just from the feel of it, even though he'd been wearing jeans.*

It was true. A bitch was in heat from some dick I hadn't even sampled yet. *But that mouth though.* I almost fumbled up the stairs as I thought about Crayson's wicked mouth because lawd, he'd had me wailing in my office like a satisfied sinner.

I walked up the few steps to the building. Scrolling through the contacts listed on the answering system, I spotted Crayson's name. Luckily, someone was leaving out of his condo, giving me the opportunity to sneak in and take a few more moments to gather my thoughts.

Based off the info I'd been told from Avery, he stayed in the penthouse suite on the top floor. Avery had said there were only two condos on the top level—Crayson's and an older lady who traveled a lot.

When I reached his door, I balanced the container I was holding on one hand and lifted my hand to knock. "Wait," I muttered as my hand froze. "What the hell am I supposed to say?" It was bad enough I was popping up at his place looking thirsty as hell, I at least needed to have a good excuse.

"Hey, I just stopped by to say thanks." I shook my head. *No, that's not good. Come up with something a little more flirtatious.*

I ran my fingers through my short cut and imagined he'd answered the door. "Hey, sexy. Want to taste my cupcakes?" I shook my head again. *Hell nah, that's too cheesy. I'm better than that.*

"So, word on the street is, you wanna fuck me." I

slapped my hand on my forehead. "Damnit. Could I sound more desperate?"

My momentary conversation with myself was cut short when the door opened. *Oh my damn.* If I hadn't already been thinking about his ass since he'd left me in my office, I would definitely have had him on my brain after seeing him answer the door. A plain white tee covered his muscular chest, giving me a great peak-a-boo of his tattooed arm sleeve. His feet were bare, and to me, there was nothing sexier than a man not afraid to show his feet. That meant he took care of himself, groomed even, and wasn't ashamed for anyone to know.

Navy blue Nike jogging pants hung low on his hips, and his five-o-clock shadow was on full display. He looked downright appetizing, but the real panty dropper was the way he was standing. Confident with his legs slightly spread to accommodate for what I already knew he was packing underneath his joggers. Although I tried to stop myself from ogling the shit out of him, I was failing and failing badly.

I almost didn't even realize he was speaking until I heard, "I appreciate the thank you. I'd love to taste your cupcakes, although I've already sampled the ones you bake as well as the sweetness in between your legs. And you're damn right, you already know I want to fuck you."

I swallowed, opening my mouth to respond to the fact that he'd obviously heard me talking to myself outside of his door, but no words came out.

"Come on in," he said, saving me the embarrassment of explaining. He stepped to the side and allowed me to step into his home. The first thing I noticed was how clean it was. It's not that I thought it would be messy, but his place appeared to be cleaner than mine.

Looking around at the tones of grey, white, and black

contemporary décor, nothing appeared to be overly decorated and his furniture wasn't overly crowded with too many chairs or sofas. Crayson seemed to be a minimalist, which surprised me since I thought he was one of those dudes who'd like to stunt on what they could afford.

I glanced over my shoulder to where he still stood in the doorway. *Jesus be a water hose* ... because I needed to be sprayed the fuck down. I swear, it was unfair for him to look so good just standing there, doing nothing.

There was only one thing he could do to make him look sexier. *Don't tuck your hands in your pockets. Don't tuck your hands in your pockets.*

"To what do I owe the pleasure of your visit?" he asked, sliding his hands into his pockets. *Shit.* The move made him look like a bad boy, yet approachable. Sexy, yet a little uncertain about my unexpected visit.

He had every right to wonder why I was here. Hell, I wondered why I was here. *Girl, quit lying. You know exactly why you're here.*

"I wanted to drop these off for you to taste," I said, referring to the container that I'd almost forgotten about. "I made them last night."

"Word!" He sounded pleasantly surprised. "I hope there's more rice crispy treats in there."

"That and more." I popped open the lid. "There's also a few cookies, cupcakes, and brownies for you to."

He took the container out my hand and walked toward the kitchen. The open floorplan of his condo was the type I'd always wanted for my place, but the real kicker was the gorgeous kitchen he had.

"Wow," I said, the word tumbling out of my mouth the minute I peeped the extremely large island and stainless steel appliances. "I'd like to think I have an amazing kitchen, but this is unreal."

He placed the container on the counter next to the refrigerator. "Thanks. I spent a lot of time working on it."

"Wait." I did a three-sixty degree turn. "You did all this?"

He shrugged. "I had some help, but yeah, I did most of it. Glad you approve."

"I more than approve." I placed my purse on one of the stools and removed my coat, revealing the maroon sweater dress I'd taken thirty minutes to pick out before leaving the house.

"Damn," he said. "You're wearing the hell out of that dress."

"Thanks." I smiled, loving that he'd noticed. Since it was still pretty damn cold out, this was one of the few dresses I had that was warm, but also fit my size twelve curvy hips in a way other dresses didn't.

"Okay, so here's the first thing I want you to try." I walked over to the container and took out the brownies I'd spent most the night perfecting. He was still standing by the container and my arm brushed his as I reached for the dessert. "There's a different kind of cocoa bean I used to make this brownie. I was worried that you'd be able to taste the weed a little more since it's a lighter type of bean, but I think I found the right balance."

I lifted the brownie to him so he could take a bite. His mouth curled around the chocolatey concoction, his lips brushing over the tips of my fingers. My eyes watched as he chewed, the act even more erotic because I knew exactly what that lethal mouth could do. The pleasure it could exude and bring me.

I moaned—yes, a bitch actually moaned—from the way

his tongue moistened his lips, savoring the last bit of brownie. I popped the rest in my mouth to give me something to do other than watching him eat. When I lifted my gaze from his mouth, his amber eyes were darker than I'd ever seen them before. *Looks like I'm not the only one affected by this moment.* Suddenly, the lustful look was replaced with concern.

"Do you want to talk about what was bothering you the other day?"

I blinked in confusion, the turn in conversation forcing me to focus on his words. "Um, sorry. That was a bad day, but I'm fine now." That was a lie. I wasn't fine by a long shot, but I didn't want to bring up that day right now. I didn't want to ruin whatever moment this was.

The reason I'd been upset that day was a much longer story than I wanted to get into right now, but luckily, I'd spent most of my life putting on a brave front in the midst of a shitty time. As much as I appreciated Crayson's concern, I didn't want it at the moment. There was only one thing on my mind. One thing I desperately needed, so I did what I do best. I put on my best fake smile and hoped like hell he didn't pick up on the fact that the demons I'd been dealing with a couple days ago were still there. Looming in the back of my mind, reminding me that I still had shit to figure out.

"I'm fine," I said, stepping closer to him. "And a large part of that is thanks to you." I pressed my hands to his chest, loving the way the softness of the cotton didn't hide how hard his body was. "Listen, you asked why I came here and I have to be honest." I took a deep breath. "It's been a while since I've felt the way I felt when you came to my office and I want to feel that again. Crayson, you claim to want to have sex with me, so I felt it only right that I stop over this morning and tell you that I want that, too." I studied his eyes, noting his surprise. "I want you to fuck me."

Now, it was his turn to study me. "How long has it been?" he asked. "Before I touched you a couple days ago, how long had it been?"

I winced. The last thing I wanted to do was own up to how long Diamond had gone without getting any male attention, yet, Crayson was clearly causing me to act unlike myself because I honestly told him, "Eighteen months. Last person was my ex and it was unmemorable to say the least."

Okay, now you're just oversharing. He didn't ask you all that. However, apparently, he liked the answer, because his eyes grew even more intense.

"Was it that joker we saw on New Year's?"

"Yeah," I answered. "That's the ex I'm talking about."

"How long were y'all together?"

"Four years. Four long ass years of my life that I can't get back."

"Four years," he repeated. "That's forty-eight months of whack ass sex." I didn't respond because he seemed to be saying it more to himself than to me. Plus, it was sad as hell that he was right. I'd gotten more pleasure from Crayson the other day than I'd ever gotten with my ex. He quirked an eyebrow. "Are you just trying to fuck me and get it out of your system? Or is this more than a one-time thing?"

I shrugged, secretly doing somersaults at the fact that he was already thinking of repeat performances when the opening act hadn't even happened yet. But I felt it only right that I make myself clear by saying, "I'm not trying to get on your damn roster or your starting lineup." He had enough bitches out here looking crazy.

"I never thought you were," he said with a laugh. "I'm just asking because I don't think one time will be enough."

His eyes roamed over me. "I like to take time with the things I cherish, and I already know your body needs to be treasured."

Oh my God. Only Crayson could say something like that and make it sound sexy as hell instead of cheesy.

"Well, in that case, if you play your cards right, maybe they'll be a repeat performance." I ran my hand over one of his tattoos. "However, the longer we stand here and talk, the less time we have to—"

I'd planned on doing a little teasing, but Crayson shut me up the minute his lips crashed over mine as he pulled me in for a delicious kiss. I could taste the brownie he'd just sampled and there was something about tasting sweet chocolate while tasting sexy chocolate that was doing crazy things to my mind. *Shit.* I wasn't even the type of bitch to enjoy kissing and whatnot. I was more of a let's-get-down-to-business sort of woman. Yet, Crayson was claiming my mouth and zapping all of my sense, and all I could do was kiss him back just as fiercely.

Without warning, he lifted me and threw me over his shoulder as if I weighed nothing. Between that kiss, the blood rushing to the front of my brain, and my heart beating fast, I was already highly stimulated and we hadn't even had sex yet. My last thought as we entered his bedroom and he tossed me on his massive California king bed was, *This is only about sex, Jordyn. Don't get addicted to some dick that isn't yours.* And it was a warning I needed to keep planted in my mind at all times.

THIRTEEN

Crayson

·

SHE'S HERE. IN MY BED. HAD ANYONE TOLD ME MONTHS ago that Jordyn Jameson would be knocking on my door, suggesting that we fuck, I would have told them to get their damn head checked. Hell, had Malakai not called and given me a heads-up that Jordyn had asked for my address, I wouldn't have been by the door to see her through the peep-hole and hear her trying to come up with excuses for her visit.

She never needed a reason to visit me. That notion should have worried me since it had been years since a chick had access to my home, but Jordyn was different. Jordyn was the type of woman who made a man change their playboy ways and settle down. That fact alone should have stopped me from bringing her to my bed, but let's be for real. What man with a working pulse would send a drop-dead beauty like Jordyn on her way without making sure she was sexually satisfied?

When she'd said, "I want you to fuck me," I'd damn near busted a nut right there. By the time I'd learned she hadn't been touched by a man in over a year and a half, I was already planning out sex positions in my head.

You've been dreaming about this. And as lame as it sounded, in my dreams, I'd pictured it happening just like this. Leaning down, I claimed her lips like I had in my kitchen, her moans singing a sweet melody in my ears. But I didn't want to hear her moan. I wanted her to scream my name and not think about whatever it was that was still bothering her. She may be able to pull all that fake shit on other people, but I knew bullshit when I saw it. Whatever Jordyn was dealing with hadn't been fixed since I'd last seen her, but she didn't need me to be her therapist right now. She needed me to treasure her body like it deserved.

I stopped kissing her long enough to take off her boots and pull her dress over her head in one quick tug. "You're beautiful," I said, stepping back to admire her lace panty and bra set that was the same color maroon as her dress.

"Alexa, play my slow jams playlist."

"Playing slow jams playlist now," Alexa said. Seconds later, a smooth hip hop song started playing through my speakers.

"I didn't think rap music would be on your slow jams playlist," Jordyn said with a smirk. "I like it."

"Rap music all day, every day." I lightly grabbed her by the ankles and tugged her toward the edge of the bed. "You still have on too many clothes." I slid her panties down her thick thighs and removed her bra, revealing a beautiful pair of brown breasts that felt as soft as they looked. I plucked one nipple into my mouth before giving the other one the same attention. She was stunning, every part of her naked body teasing me with a promise that no part was better than the other. She was a work of art—soft, yet firm; plush, yet tight. To make it simple, she was my perfect woman. Thick in all of the right places with the confidence that let others know she knew she looked damn good and was proud of every curve she had.

Her skin tasted like a sweet peaches dipped in a brown sugar glaze, and whatever perfume or lotion she was wearing had me ready to eat her whole. I stood back up to remove my T-shirt and jogging pants, enjoying the way her eyes followed my every move.

"It's beautiful," she whispered, sitting up from the bed, wrapping her soft hands around my dick. I'd already been semi-hard before she'd touched me, but now, I was growing to full alert, her hands and the look in her eyes not helping the situation. I needed to make this last as long as I could, and based off the way she'd licked her lips, I needed to take back control before I busted my load before I got a chance to bury myself inside of her.

"Lean back down," I told her. "There will be time for that later." She listened, but I didn't miss the hint of regret reflected in her gaze.

I started kissing the insides of her thighs, ready to taste her sweet pussy again, but she stopped me. "Like you said, there's time for that later." In a move I hadn't expected, she pushed me down to the bed and straddled me, her pussy landing on my dick with purpose. I was too surprised to stop her hips from grinding on me to the beat of the music, so I grabbed her waist and moved my hips along with hers.

Shit. I hadn't dry-humped in forever, and even when I used to back when I was a teenager, it had never felt this damn good. This wasn't usually how I operated. I had no problem releasing control, but that was usually after I'd done things my way first. Most women went along with how I did things. *But Jordyn isn't any woman.* Nah, she was different, and although I wanted to take it slow, she was moving her luscious body in a way that was letting it be known that she was in charge.

Though it wouldn't take much for me to take back the control, I reminded myself that she needed this. It was still the morning time, so I bet that she'd woken up needing this release and I was lucky bastard who got to give her exactly what she needed. We'd already established this wasn't a one-time thing, so I could worship her body the way I wanted later. For now, I'd give her what she desired.

"Tell me what you want," I asked, halting her hips to grab a condom and slip it on before we went any further. "Tell me how you want it."

"I don't want it slow the first time," she said breathlessly, her hips moving again now that the condom was in place. "I want it hard. Fast. Dirty. I want you to fuck me like this is the only chance you'll get." With that, she lifted her hips and angled her body right over my dick before she slid me into her slick pussy quicker than I'd anticipated. The feel of her heat wrapped about me in a tight embrace made me stop the movement of her hips so I could enjoy the feeling.

I looked up into her face, her wicked smile just as satisfied as I felt. She pushed my hands away and started riding my dick to the beat of another song.

"Fuckkkkk." She was gonna be the death of me. I was sure of it. If she wanted it hard and dirty, then damnit, I was going to give the woman what she wanted. I waited until the song was over before I grabbed her by the waist and changed our position, lifting her left leg as I did so.

My dick never left her heat, but the move gave me

better access to her pussy. "Holy shit," she yelled, her legs already shaking from the orgasm that I knew would be hitting her soon. Using my free hand, I placed my thumb on her clit, circling around her numb in a way I knew would drive her crazy.

"Fuck. Fuck. Fuck. Fuck. Fuck."

I laughed at the curse words flying out of her mouth. Some women would be too embarrassed to yell out curse words because they felt like it gave a man too much power to know he was affecting her, but I never understood that shit. Great dick should make a woman curse or start speaking in tongue, just like great pussy made a man do the same damn thing. It was nothing to be embarrassed about. If anything, it was something to be celebrated because not everyone enjoyed sex.

And Jordyn? Jordyn didn't just have great pussy. Her shit was phenomenal. The type of pussy a dude like me got hooked on. The type of pussy that changed a man, because as good as he'd had it before, she'd proven you hadn't been having the best. She was the best and he was an idiot if he thought there was pussy in the world that was better than this.

"I'm close," she murmured, her forehead damp with perspiration from their current morning activity. I didn't respond, but instead, angled myself even more which brought me in even deeper, while my thumb continued to work its magic. Seconds later, she released an orgasm so strong, she started cursing even more. I waited for her convulsions to subside before I succumbed to the orgasm I'd been holding onto since she'd walked through my door. It was powerful, just as I'd suspected.

"That was ... amazing," Jordyn said, the lust in her voice still fucking with me. *She sounds so damn good.* A pissed off

Jordyn was great, but an aroused Jordyn? There was nothing like it.

"I agree." I placed a quick kiss on her lips. "That was amazing." I got off the bed and went to my connecting bathroom to discard the condom. When I returned, I expected her to have gotten under the sheets or start putting on her clothes, but that wasn't the case. Instead, she was on her side, her head leaning into her hand, looking sexier than a woman had a right to look.

"Uh, can we do it again?" she asked, her seductive eyes pulling me in. "Hard and fast like before?" Her eyes roamed over my naked body. "I'd love to hit that again before I open my bar."

I laughed as I shook my head. "I'm beginning to think all I am is a piece of meat to you."

She slightly frowned. "Is that a problem for you?"

Being used? By Jordyn Jameson? The answer was easy. "Hell nah." Her smile widened, the crook of her finger motioning for me to join her on the bed. I ignored the voice in the back of my head that told me I had to be careful. Jordyn was addictive ... in more ways than one.

FOURTEEN

Jordyn

"Damn, girl. Early in the morning? You're such a hussy." Avery playfully hit me on the shoulder.

"How Sway?" I asked, feigning ignorance

She rolled her eyes. "Knocking on his door for early morning D, that's how."

"Shhh, lower your voice."

Avery glanced around the bar. "Sorry, I'm just happy that you finally let Crayson clear out those cobwebs. I was hoping that's why you needed his address."

After having sex with Crayson most of the day yesterday, I'd had been too tired to call Avery. Per usual, she'd been staying at Malakai's place, but I should have known that the minute I told her, she'd bring her ass to my bar itching for details.

"Let's go sit at our table." I nodded to the corner that

had become our favorite spot before giving my bartender, Greg, a nod so he knew to cover things.

"Ohh, good," Avery blurted, following me to the table. "Tell me the details before Ty and Serenity get here."

I took a seat in my favorite chair that also had the best view of the door. *Girl, be for real. That's not your favorite seat. You just hope Crayson's fine ass walks past the window on his way in or out of his cigar lounge.* I knew he'd be working at Undefined Sanctum today because he'd told me yesterday that he'd made great progress on creating access to the private room. I couldn't remember the last time someone believed in one of my dreams enough to put forth so much effort.

I took a sip of my water and tried to will my eyes away from staring a hole in his building. "What do you want to know?"

"What do I want to know!" Avery shook my arm. "I want to know everything. Malakai didn't have any details." Her hands flew to her mouth as soon as she said the statement.

"You're kidding me," I said. "Malakai told you before I did? Meaning, Crayson told him. That sucka. I told him not to tell Malakai."

Avery looked at me with confusion written across her face. "Why did you tell him that? You were already planning on telling me, so you had to know he'd tell his brother. That man has been after you for months."

"Exactly. I wanted to tell you first, which is the only reason I asked him not to say anything. I didn't want news to travel so fast. But Crayson didn't know why. I was testing him."

"You mean playing games with him."

I shrugged. "Same difference."

"Not really." Avery waved her hands in the air. "Anyway, we're getting off topic. What I want to know is how are you even functioning with all that great sex you had?"

I shrugged. "Who said he was great in bed?"

Avery gave me a full eye roll complete with a lip smack. "Girl, please. I know you playin'. You're walking with a slight limp, so I know he laid it on you yesterday."

I tried to hide my smile, but it was no use. She was right. My thighs and legs were sorer than they'd ever been, which was saying a lot since I once let one of my bartenders talk me into doing a ten-mile run. That shit was downright exhausting, but it still didn't compare to Crayson.

I groaned, hating that I was about to admit, "It was better than great. Probably the best I ever had."

Avery leaned back and braced her hands on the table. "Dayum, it's like that! I guess it's true what they say."

"What do they say?" I questioned.

She grinned. "That the Madden brothers are all beasts in the bedroom. I know Malakai is, and last time I was in Arkansas, the women in town had plenty to say about Caden. Malik and Micah's wives seem plenty satisfied and have kids to show for it. And although I haven't heard much about Carter, I bet the apple doesn't fall far from the tree."

"It's doesn't," Serenity said as she approached the table with Ty right by her side. Those two were peas in a pod. *Crap, I didn't even see them walk in.* I'd hoped to get a few more minutes alone with Avery before the entire brigade walked in.

"Oh, is that so, Serenity?" Avery wiggled her eyebrows. "It's about damn time you shared some juicy details about Carter. Is he really that great in the bedroom?"

Her face flushed. "Uh, what? What do you mean? Why would I know that about him?"

Avery glanced to me and Ty before looking back at Serenity. "Because you walked up and confirmed that the apple doesn't fall far from the tree, and I was just saying that the Madden brothers all seem to be good in bed."

Serenity shook her head. "I didn't know that's what you were talking about. I thought you were talking about their good looks or something."

Ty snickered. "Sis, Crayson, Caden, and Carter are triplets, so we already know that. I figured they were talking about sex when we walked up."

Serenity started fidgeting with her fingers, a sure sign she didn't want to continue the conversation. I didn't know much about her past relationship with Carter, but clearly, there was a story there.

"Girl, would you calm down. This conversation isn't about you." Ty placed his hands over Serenity's fingers and turned to look me dead in the eye. "If Avery and Jordyn were talking about sex, it's obvious that Jordyn finally fornicated."

Shit. How did he guess that? Ty always seemed to be guessing some shit that folks didn't want to share.

My eyes narrowed. "Seriously? Fornicated? You couldn't find a better word?"

"Yeah, it's a pretty strange way to say it," Avery said.

Serenity nodded. "Agreed. You could have just said sex."

"Damn," Ty blurted. "Can't a bitch say an educated word without the grammar police getting all uptight about word usage."

I laughed, hoping he'd drop it, but knowing that was a long shot. He proved me right when he asked, "Are you going to supply the details, or should we pretend you and

Crayson didn't finally have sex and ask Avery to spill the tea to us later?"

"You have no chill."

Ty clasped his hands on the table. "And you are terrible at diverting the attention away from you, so spill, boo. Did you finally let that sexy man and all his asshole glory tap that ass?"

I couldn't help but laugh, as did Avery and Serenity. Ty always managed to say things less than poetic. I slightly groaned. "Is there anything I can do to get you to drop this?"

"Yes," he claimed, nodding his head. "First, own up to it. You know the minute we see you and Crayson in the same room, we'll be able to tell."

"Fine," I moaned. "Yes, we had sex."

"Now, tell us if his pride and joy is the size of a slim banana or the size of a thick cucumber. And is he more of a care bear or a tommy taker?"

"Thick, big cucumber," I said, failing at keeping flashes of him thrusting inside of me out of my mind. "And he's definitely more of a giver than a taker."

"Eeek." Avery clapped her hands together. "I knew it."

"One last thing." Ty leaned closer and lowered his voice. "Is he more of a Barack Obama type of lover or is the Kevin Hart vibe more his speed?"

"What?" I gasped. "What does that even mean?"

He snorted. "You know what I mean. Barack Obama has that black man swag. He walks slow, purposeful. Like his own soundtrack is playing in the background with every step. And his voice is melodic. Influential. Kevin Hart is a comedian, so he talks like he's always setting you up for a punch line. Plus, he's always yell-screaming, which probably means his lovemaking is, well, opposite of Obama."

"I get it, but that's a messed up analogy," Serenity said.

"It's like you're asking Jordyn if having sex with Crayson was more like sleeping with Obama or Kevin Hart."

"That's exactly what I'm asking." Ty waved his hands to the group. "Are y'all telling me that y'all never thought about fucking either one of those men?"

Avery rolled her eyes. "Really, Ty? No, I haven't. I admire our prior president, and he will always be my president, but I never thought about having sex with him. And Kevin Hart makes me laugh, but he's just ... small."

"Girl, please." Ty glanced between the three of us to make sure we heard his argument. "Obama had all of the ladies and us fabulous men wondering what him and Michelle did in their spare time. You know he's probably a good lover based off how he walks. Hell, he's gotta be doing something to keep Michelle happy. She's a boss bitch. And like I said, that voice?" He fanned himself. "Every time Obama speaks in that smooth, strong voice, he drips of power and naughty sentiments. On the other end, Kevin Hart always walks fast as if he's being chased or trying to overcompensate for his height. It's as if his swiftness is trying to prove that his short legs don't mean he walks slow. Or fucks slow. Little does he know, that makes us see him as a quick shooter. Sometimes, you want that. A good quickie."

I blinked, not even knowing how the conversation got here. "I'm gonna pass on answering that and just conclude by saying that Crayson definitely knows what he's doing in the bedroom." They didn't need to know all of my business. A bitch had to have some damn secrets. "And y'all betta not make this a topic of conversation outside of today because I'm not trying to make things weird between us." I knew that was asking the impossible, because with this group, tea was always being spilled. Plus, I knew Avery and I would still talk about it. However, this way, maybe it wouldn't be brought up every time we were together.

"Okay," Serenity said.

Avery gave me a look that said not really, but told me, "Sure."

"Hell nah," Ty blurted. "I won't bring it up all the time, but come on, you know it's getting brought up again, right?"

Just as I was about to address Ty, I saw movement in front of Crayson's building through the window. He was wearing blue jeans and a black pea coat, and from the looks of it, his brothers were with him.

Avery followed my line of vision and explained, "They are in town for our engagement party tomorrow night. They came a day early to hang out with Malakai and Crayson."

It seemed all of the Madden brothers were present except for Carter. *Hmm, I wonder if he's going to show them what he's doing in the basement.* No sooner had the thought left my mind did I dismiss it. Granted, I'd chosen to confide in Crayson because I needed to get him on board about the private underground room connecting our properties, but I still trusted him to keep my secret. *And you already trusted him with your body, so maybe he can handle a few more secrets ...* The thought shocked me because I'd spent most of my life keeping things to myself and not entrusting others with information I held near and dear to my heart. It was a strange feeling to actually want to share more with Crayson. Especially more than I'd already shared.

"Ladies, I do believe the Madden bug has bit our dear Jordyn straight in her feisty ass."

I turned to an amused Ty before seeing Serenity and Avery wearing matching sympathetic smiles. The last thing I needed was to get addicted to a man like Crayson. Yeah, he may have been the one to give me the best sex of my life, but I was just caught up in the moment, right? The feeling had to pass.

"Nah, it won't," Serenity said. Ty and Avery were onto another topic, but Serenity was looking solely at me.

I squinted my eyes. "I didn't say anything."

She shrugged. "You didn't need to. I'd know that look a mile away. Crayson has you all in your feelings, so you're probably hoping it's just a phase and will fade after time. But take my word sis, once a Madden gets under your skin, it's hard to get rid of him. My advice? Enjoy it while you can and take it for what it's worth."

I focused on her, once again wishing that I knew the story between her and Carter, which was strange because I wasn't even the nosey type. I didn't even have to ask Avery to confirm because Serenity's eyes told it all. Getting over any man with the last name Madden was going to take a lot more than wishful thinking.

Shit. I was fucked.

FIFTEEN

Crayson

A hundred people at the party, yet only one brown-skinned siren is on my mind. It was finally the night of Malakai and Avery's engagement party, and even though Undefined Sanctum's first unveiling was going off without a hitch, I couldn't get my mind off Jordyn.

"I'm proud of you, brother," Malakai said, slapping my shoulder. "Out of all your cigar lounges, this one is my favorite."

I smiled in pride at my brother's words. I'd put a lot of blood, sweat, and tears into making sure Undefined Sanctum surpassed the hype of Unclassified Hideaway and Unsettled Retreat.

"Thanks, bruh. After tonight, I'm even more ready for the official grand opening in a month." Having Malakai and Avery's family and close friends, along with a few of my elite cigar members who'd joined with the promise that this cigar lounge would be my most exclusive, was a huge plus. I was able to hear what people liked and disliked in plenty of time to make adjustments.

I nodded to Malakai. "How about you get Pops and the fellas so we can head to my largest private cigar suite."

"For sho'. I think Jordyn has some of the family partici-pating in some sort of engagement celebration game, but I'll round them up."

I laughed. "You're the groom. Why the hell are you with me and not playing the damn game?"

Malakai glanced around, as if not wanting anyone to overhear. "Nigga, I didn't even want this engagement party, but you insisted and I figured you wanted a reason to plan something with Jordyn, so I agreed. But all I want to do is marry that woman standing over there." He nodded toward Avery who was engrossed in whatever game Jordyn had come up with.

"I feel you." I looked Jordyn's way and caught her eye. For a beat, something passed between us and I immediately recognized what it was on my end. My body was still itching to touch that juicy ass that was jiggling underneath her black dress every time she walked.

"You good?" Malakai asked with a knowing look.

"Yeah." I dropped eye contact with Jordyn and turned to Malakai. "Thanks for looking out, big bro."

"No problem. I think y'all look good together."

"We aren't together," I said a little too quickly.

"Right," he deadpanned. "Let me find the guys. I know they're prolly hiding so they don't have to participate in this game."

"Bet. I'll set up first." I walked to the hallway that led to the private suites, proud of myself for having the foresight to build these private cigar suites. Folks attending the party were already making reservations and paying some good coins for them.

When I made it to the largest suite, I went to unlock the safe where I'd previously placed some limited Cuban cigars that cost $500 a cigar and had a hint of cognac for flavor. I wanted my brothers and dad to be the first to try these one of a kind cigars.

"This is nice," a voice said from behind me. "I think you'll get a lot of reservations for this space."

I turned to see Jordyn standing in the entryway of the suite. *Damn.* She looked even better up close. I could tell she'd just gotten her hair done because her edgy cut looked fresh, but what really had me bugging was this burgundy lipstick she was wearing that was the same color as her fuck-me heels.

"Especially since it has frosted windows." She pursed her lips. "Even more privacy."

"Thanks. I'll have to give you a private tour of all of the perks at another time. The guys and I are about to check out these cigars soon." I continued to look her up and down. "Was there anything you needed before they get here?"

"Yeah," she said, closing the door and twisting the lock. My eyes went to her ass, unable to help myself with her in such close quarters.

She sauntered toward me, her eyes laser focused on mine. "I had fun the other day. I needed that."

"Me too." I cleared my throat when she stopped right in front of me. "I hadn't wanted you to leave." *Shit.* I winced at my honesty. Although it was the truth, I wasn't tryin' to tell her all that. She already had a hold on me.

She smiled slyly, playing with the lapels of my blazer

before placing her hands on my chest. "You know what else I've been thinking about?" Her voice was low. *Sultry.*

I swallowed. "What?"

"About that thing you do," she whispered. "With your tongue."

"Real ... Really?" I wanted to say more, but her body and scent were turning me into one of those one-word, stuttering mutha fucka's.

"Yeah." Her hands moved farther down until they were cupping my dick through my jeans. "Made me realize I never showed you what I can do with my tongue."

Holy shit. If her goal was to shock the hell out of me, it was working. "I'll have to test out your tongue action some time soon."

"Or now," she suggested. I didn't even have a chance to respond because she'd dropped to her knees and unzipped my jeans in record timing.

"Ah." The response died on my tongue the minute her burgundy lips wrapped around my dick, the suction causing me to brace myself on the nearby wall. "Shit, Jordyn." I may sound like an asshole by saying the woman knew how to down a dick like the only way for her to get through the night was sucking me whole, but it was true. She licked and gripped with the perfect amount of pressure and speed, her warm, wet tongue making it hard for me to hold back my groans. I couldn't believe I was seconds away from busting a nut so fast, but just as those sensations started to rise, she plopped my dick out of her mouth and stood up.

She straightened her dress, and with a wicked smile, she told me, "I have to get back to the party."

"Woman, what the hell. You tryin' to give me blue balls?"

Her eyes sparkled as she crossed her arms over her

chest. "I told you not to tell Malakai we had sex, but you didn't listen. So yeah, giving you blue balls was the plan."

"You've got to be fucking kidding me," I muttered. "I saw you talking to Avery, Ty, and Serenity at your bar yesterday. Are you telling me you didn't tell them anything? Cause Ty has been winking at me all damn night."

She shrugged. "Maybe I did, maybe I didn't. But the rule was, you couldn't say anything. I never promised the same." With that, she turned and sashayed out of the suite, her confident stride making me shake my head.

In the hallway, I heard my brothers and dad, so I figured Malakai had rounded up the crew. Meaning, I'd have to get revenge on Jordyn at another time. I laughed to myself as I lifted my dick so the guys couldn't tell I was hard as hell, and zipped back up my jeans.

"Fucking tease." She was being ridiculous, but I'd already known Jordyn liked to play games. Hell, I liked them myself sometimes.

Her antics kept things interesting, but there was no way I was letting her get away with that shit. If she thought I was one of these lame ass niggas who let her run shit and do whatever she wanted, she had another thing coming.

Jordyn

"What did you do to him?" Avery asked.

"Yeah, he's seemed torn between cursing you out and eye fucking you all night," Serenity added.

"Uh, hmm," Ty said. "And based off the way he's been walking for the past few hours, his dick is hard." We all turned to look at Ty. "What?" He lifted his arms in defense. "Don't hate on me because I notice shit."

Now that the engagement party was over, the crew was all at a brand new club that had opened a couple blocks away from my bar and Crayson's cigar shop. Crayson had been shaking his head at me for most of the night, but now, he was looking downright dangerous with the looks he was shooting my way.

Was I wrong for making Crayson hard right before the guys came into the private cigar suite? A little. Had I enjoyed every moment of it? Hell yeah.

I turned toward the bar and ordered a cocktail. I wasn't really in a drinking mood, but I needed something to take the edge off. After I'd gotten my drink, we made our way to the dance floor as one of our jams came on. I could dance my ass off, although I rarely got the chance to hit up a club anymore. As I wound my hips to the beat and sang along with my friends, I could feel him watching my every move. The thing I was learning the most about Crayson was that surprisingly, despite all of the shit-talking he did, he was strategic in his moves. I hadn't missed him calling me a fucking tease as I'd exited the private cigar suite earlier, but for the past few hours, he hadn't done a damn thing about it.

And you want him to do something about it. As wrong as it sounded, I liked watching him sweat, and if I happened to push his limit by shamelessly flirting, then leaving him high and dry, so be it.

Another song came on, and I twisted my hips even more in a slow grind. I glanced over at Crayson, satisfied to find him watching me.

"You ain't shit," Avery whispered. "He's watching you hard."

"That's the plan," I whispered back, before I dipped my hips a little more, making sure that I didn't overdo it. Some dance moves were better left understated.

"He's coming this way," Serenity warned. I glanced over my shoulder and confirmed that he was. And by the looks of it, he was done playing eye-tag.

"Come with me." He grabbed my hand, pulling me in the opposite direction of our friends.

"Wait, my drink is about to spill."

"Forget that shit." Grabbing it out of my hand, he placed it on a nearby high table. The loud thump made the women standing by the table jump, until they caught sight of Crayson, before their eyes met mine in a knowing look.

"Get it, girl," one of them said. Typically, I wasn't one to blast what I did between the sheets to any damn body, but Crayson was clearly making me act brand fucking new because instead of brushing it off, I yelled, "I will," as we reached the back of the club.

We turned two corners and made it to a spiral staircase that he started to descend. I was surprised I was even able to keep up with him at the speed he was walking. I didn't have a clue as to where we were going, but I couldn't have been more surprised when we reached an empty storage room in the basement.

"We probably shouldn't be down here," I said, glancing around at all of the supplies.

"I know the owner," Crayson replied. "I found some rare cigars for him to give some of his elite and frequent club patrons, so he owes me a favor." He backed me into a wall, a chill running down my spine in anticipation.

If someone would have told me last year that I'd be

ready and willing to fuck the shit out of Crayson Madden, I would have told them to get their damn head checked. "What if we get caught?"

He grinned in a way that had me holding my breath. "You think too damn much." And just like that, his determined lips were on mine, while his hands were roaming over any part of my body he could reach.

"You've been fucking with me all day," he said in between kisses. "Walking around in that tight ass dress, flaunting your thick thighs in my face while you danced. Making my dick hard." In one swift move, he lifted my dress to my waist, and pulled down my thong. "Time for your punishment."

He dropped to his knees, threw my left leg over his shoulder, and swirled his tongue around my clit, making Diamond very, *very* happy. The man had a tongue that was made for pleasuring women and I wasn't ashamed of the fact that he had me squirming on the wall.

When I was close to coming, he stood up and unzipped his pants, sliding his dick into my slick heat with precision. *That feels so damn good.* We'd had the talk about being clean and not using condoms before the second round the last time we'd had sex. It was reckless as hell, but hey, that's why they made birth control, right? Besides, I refused to think about how crazy it was that I'd gone eighteen months without having sex, yet, I was already craving Crayson after twenty-four hours of him sexing me like crazy.

My moans mingled with his groans as our sounds filled the cramped space. I was close again. On the brink of experiencing the type of awe-inspiring orgasm that I'd only experienced recently with Crayson. When he lifted to bring his dick even deeper, I bit into his shoulder, unable to handle the amount of pleasure I was experiencing. All day, I'd been waiting for him to fuck me, yet, just when I started shaking as my orgasm grew even nearer, he lowered my leg and pulled out.

My eyes were still focused solely on his beautiful, long dick that was winking at me, anxious to get back inside when I asked, "What are you doing?"

"Wrapping it up to get back to the party," he answered, zipping his pants back up. "You should know by now, not to play games with a man like me."

I blinked, trying to slow my heart rate. *You've got to be shitting me. He's not serious.* Yet, seeing the sly expression on his face, I knew he meant it. He wasn't giving me the orgasm he knew I needed. *Desired.* My irritation rose by the second.

"What in the ever-living fuck, Crayson?" I didn't care if the whole damn club heard me when I told him, "I didn't give you permission to remove your dick from my pussy. So, you're gonna finish what you started and give me a damn orgasm. *Now.*" I was heated and it wasn't only in the lustful way.

He had the nerve to look unaffected, crossing his arms over his chest to tell me, "No, I'm not."

I'm gonna kill him. "You're a goddamn asshole."

His eyes darkened. "An asshole you still want to fuck right now." He placed a quick kiss on my lips and I punched him in the arm, hating that I'd wished the kiss had been longer. With a smirk I wanted to slap off his damn face, he went back up the stairs, leaving me in that crowded ass basement.

I stomped back up the stairs annoyed as hell. I said good-bye to our friends, still annoyed as hell. I took an Uber home, cursing his ass the entire way and not caring if the driver was getting irritated at hearing my voice.

Despite my frustration, when I reached my place, I walked straight into my bedroom and pulled out my vibrator. Crayson Madden may infuriate me, but a bitch was still horny as hell, so if I couldn't have the real thing, I was damn sure masturbating to my memories.

SIXTEEN

Jordyn

"LET'S GET THIS SHIT OVER WITH," I SAID TO MYSELF AS I glanced at the clock. Tonight, Crayson was coming over to help me finish making some more desserts for that large order and I couldn't be less excited. So far, my client had loved everything I'd sent to them, but that wasn't the reason for my bad mood. Nope. My bad mood could be contributed all to Crayson and the way he'd left me in that basement a couple days ago.

When he'd called me this morning to remind me that we'd made plans to get together and bake, I'd almost cursed his ass out and told him to lose my number. Then I realized I was just being a little dramatic and the best thing for me to do would be to act like he wasn't affecting me.

The knock on the door startled me from my thoughts. Opening the door, I reminded myself to breathe and ignore the fact that Crayson looked even sexier than he did when I last saw him. *That's because you've missed the bastard.* He was rocking a five-o'-clock shadow again and my fingers itched to touch the coarse hair.

"Come on in," I said. "I baked the first couple batches. Now, I have everything set up for the next two, so we can get started right away."

He followed me back to my kitchen, my heart rate racing out of nerves. *Come on, girl, you've been with him alone plenty of times by now. Just chill.*

"Okay, first things first. I need you to prep the pans." I pointed to the pans on the counter, while Crayson placed a bag he'd been holding down, next to the pans.

"I made dinner," he said, pulling out a variety of containers from the bag.

"Dinner?" My nose was already twitching in delight at the aroma of food when he popped open the lids.

"I figured you'd be so busy baking all day, you wouldn't have time to eat. So I made some sirloin tips, broccoli, and an alfredo pasta for us." He went over to my cabinets and got out some plates and silverware, before taking a seat on one of my stools.

Still a little bit surprised, I took the seat right next to him while he placed food on our plates. "This all smells so delicious."

He smiled. "I hope it tastes delicious, too."

It didn't take long after he'd handed me my plate for me to dig in. "Oh my God, it tastes even better than it smells."

"Thank you," he said, catching my eyes. "You work too hard. Someone should be taking care of you."

I stopped swallowing, his words affecting me more than they should have. *By someone, does he mean him?* Making me dinner didn't mean our ... whatever we were, was anything serious, but it felt nice to hear him say those words. For him to want to take care of me if only for one night. *Not true, girl. That naughty mouth of his took care of your horny ass over a week ago. That's how you ended up in this predicament in the first place.*

I sighed, trying not to eye-fuck him while he chewed, but failing miserably. His tongue was just *nasty* in the best way possible, which meant, eating while keeping my legs closed was damn near impossible.

Somehow, I managed. We ate in a comfortable silence, both of us not too eager to spoil the moment with words. Once we'd finished, Crayson gathered our dirty dishes and placed them in the dishwasher.

"Okay, now I'm ready to get my hands dirty," he said, rubbing his hands together. "Where do you want me?"

Although he was talking about baking, his words were planting all sorts of dirty thoughts in my mind. Just as I was about to respond to him, my cell phone rang.

I glanced down at the caller I.D. "Sorry, I have to get this."

"No worries." He started prepping the pans as I answered.

"Hey, Grandpa, what's up?"

"Hey, Jordy," Grandpa said. "It's time for us to finish that talk."

I sighed. My grandpa was the only one who'd ever called me Jordy, at least anymore ... "I know, Grandpa, but my answer is still the same. I don't want to come home to Maine. I think I'll pass."

"You can't pass on this, Jordy," he said. "It's been over seven years. It's time for you to come home and face this like the woman you were raised to be."

I pinched the bridge of my nose, the signs of a headache

already coming on. "Gramps, I can't do this now. I'll have to call you back later."

"Okay, Jordy," he said in a frustrated tone. "It's been too long since you've been home, but I won't force you. Call me when you can."

"Love you, Gramps."

"Love you, too."

I hung up with my grandfather, only then noticing the concerned expression on Crayson's face.

"Is everything okay?"

Tell him it's not. Tell him you haven't been fine since your grandfather started calling you weeks ago. Maybe even before that. As badly as I wanted to tell him the truth, I squared my shoulders and told him, "I'm fine. Just some family stuff."

He seemed unconvinced. "Are you sure? It sounds like your grandpa was trying to get you to go back home."

"He was." I started helping Crayson with the pans. "I haven't been back home in seven years."

"Since you moved to New York?" he asked.

"Yeah. I left Maine and never looked back." *More like, you were too hurt to look back.*

I wasn't looking his way, but I could feel his eyes on me, observing my behavior. "When does your grandfather want you to come home?"

"The day after tomorrow," I replied. "There's an important event that he wants me to attend."

He walked over to my side of the counter. "Jordyn, I'm not sure what's going on or why you haven't been home in seven years, but I'll go with you if you want to go back home and need a little support."

My head flew up to meet his gaze. I had to have heard

him wrong. "Are you offering to go back to my hometown with me?"

"That's exactly what I'm offering."

My mouth parted. "You mean that?"

His hand lightly touched my chin. "Of course."

My heartbeat quickened, the overwhelming feeling of what he was suggesting placing a heavy weight on my shoulders. For years, I'd done things on my own, never relying on anyone more than what I was comfortable with. Yet, here I was, relying on Crayson in ways I never had with anyone before. I couldn't lie, the feeling was a little unsettling, but even more than that, it felt nice to trust someone again. I opened my mouth, prepared to thank him for his offer, but politely decline. Instead, the next words I blurted were, "Thank you, I'd love to take you up on your offer. Like my grandfather told me, I've been away from home for too long."

He seemed as surprised that I'd agreed as I was, but soon, we were discussing our schedules and flight details, while making a few calls for our staff to cover things while we were away. It wasn't until we'd finally gotten back to baking that I'd realized the grave mistake I'd made. Up until now, I hadn't told Crayson much about my family. He didn't know how I was raised. He wasn't aware of the kind of childhood I'd had. He was in the dark about the adversity that I still had to overcome.

No one in New York knew about my life back in Maine, not even my ex or Avery. I had to be honest with Crayson before we arrived. There was no other way around it.

There were hundreds of reasons why I shouldn't take Crayson back to my hometown. Yet, for every one of those reasons, I could only think of the reason why I should. One reason why taking Crayson back home was a good decision.

With him, you feel the most yourself. The most like the Jordyn behind the pain and hurt. There was something about Crayson that made me feel like I didn't have to hide who I truly was. Deep down, I knew I should take the time to figure out why that was, but I wasn't. At least not tonight.

Crayson

SHE WAS NERVOUS ABOUT SOMETHING, BUT SHE DIDN'T want to talk about it. That much I could tell. Our flight had landed in Portland an hour ago and we'd already gotten our bags and rental car.

When I'd first told Malakai that I was going to Maine to visit Jordyn's family, he'd been shocked as hell and rightfully so. I hadn't shown this much interest in a woman since Danielle, and even then, we'd never met each other's families. Our relationship hadn't been like that.

That night I'd been at Jordyn's, I'd surprised myself by offering to go with her back home, and I'd been even more surprised when she'd agreed. Seeing the hurt reflected in her eyes had hit me square in the heart. I'd wanted to find a way to support her when she was obviously struggling with whatever was bothering her. It had been the same look I'd seen in her eyes the night I'd visited her in her office.

"We're only thirty minutes away," she said when we hit the highway. "Are you sure you're okay with staying in my grandfather's home?"

"Yeah, I'm good. My parents always make us stay at

their B&B when we're in town. Either there, or at Caden's ranch. So I'm used to staying with family instead of hotels."

"Great. I didn't tell him we were coming, but he'll be thrilled and want us to stay with him." She smiled, but the smile didn't quite reach her eyes. We rode in silence for most of the ride, and something told me that Jordyn needed the quiet. She hadn't been home in over seven years, so there had to be a good reason for that.

Unlike most women who wanted to engross me in every aspect of their life, Jordyn wasn't anything like that. Granted, she'd let me in on a big secret of hers, but she'd been calculated in her approach. She'd only told me what she felt like I needed to know, similar to what she'd expressed about her family. I didn't want to push her, because I knew she'd talk when she was ready.

When we pulled in front of a large, brown brick home, she opened her purse and pulled out a picture of three people. "This is my family," she said.

I took the picture in my hand. "Is this your grandfather and parents?"

"Yeah." She stared at the picture, a faraway look in her eyes. "I've never told this to anyone, not even Avery. She's always been curious about my family, but even my social media pages are mainly about my bar. I don't have anything on them that's personal."

I knew this much already because I was man enough to admit that I'd snooped through her Facebook and Instagram pages a few times. Besides her bar and a few pictures of her and Avery, she was right. She didn't put much up.

"Avery knows part of the story, but not everything. She dropped the topic once she saw how emotional it made me." She glanced up from the photo and looked me in my eyes. "I guess there's no easy way to say it, so I'll just rip off the

Band-Aid. My parents died a little over seven years ago, and the day after their funeral, I packed up what I could from my bedroom and moved to New York. I haven't looked back since."

Damn. I reached across the car's console and placed my hand over hers. I hadn't expected her tell me that. "I'm so sorry to hear that. I can't even begin to imagine how you feel." Yeah, my parents may annoy me sometimes, but I couldn't imagine one of them not being here.

"I'm okay for the most part," she said with a shrug. She glanced out the window to the house before looking back to me. "Actually, I take that back. I'm not okay. The reason my grandfather has been begging me to come home is because my parents were influential in the community. My dad was mayor of our small Portland neighborhood and my mom was a beloved high school teacher. They both valued education and every year since they've passed, the community has had a memorial for them in which ten lucky students get academic scholarships in their honor. This year, they want me to speak at the awards ceremony."

I continued to rub her hand, my heart aching for her loss. She didn't want to be back here. She didn't want to be in Maine. Yet, the struggle in her facial features was that of a person who felt guilty that they'd been away for so long. "I know it may be difficult, but something tells me that your parents would have wanted you to be here when you were ready. So maybe you shouldn't focus on how long it took you to get here, but the fact that you finally came. That's saying something."

"It sure is," she replied with a forced laugh. "It's saying that I'm a selfish bitch who would rather avoid her problems than tackle them head on. I may have finally decided to come, but now I'm stalling because I don't want to get out of the car. This neighborhood holds too many memories for me ... more bad than good. Besides my grandfather and a few others, I'm not even sure anyone in town will be excited to see me."

I shook my head, my words clear when I told her, "I don't know the entire story, only what you've just told me. However, no one can put a time limit on how long it takes you to grieve. So if seven years is how long it took for you to come home, you're entitled to that time."

Her head turned toward the door of the house. "Looks like my time just ran out."

I followed her line of vision, my eyes landing on an older gentleman who was standing in the open doorway, leaning on his cane. He looked like the man in the picture, which meant it was her grandfather.

He began walking toward the car, his eyes focused and inquisitive like he was trying to figure out who was in the car. I was still watching him when Jordyn stepped out of our rental and began walking toward her grandfather. His eyes lit up when he recognized her, careful steps turning rushed as he dropped his cane and limped toward Jordyn. I stepped out of the car, but I stood back to let them have a moment alone.

I couldn't see Jordyn's face, but based off how her pace quickened, I knew she was just as moved to see him as he was her.

"My JayJay," he said, his voice full of emotion as they hugged. "You came home. You finally came home."

I approached slowly, not wanting my Timberland boots to clunk on the concrete pavement and break the moment. Her grandfather's eyes studied me as he broke their hug and pushed his granddaughter behind him.

"We don't need any trouble, young man. So get yo' ass

on." His voice was firm. Direct. I wasn't surprised by his reaction. Being six-foot-three and two-hundred and sixty pounds of tatted muscle, I was used to folks assuming I was up to no good.

"Grandpa, this is my friend, Crayson." Jordyn walked over to me and gently tugged me toward her grandfather. "Crayson, this is my grandfather, Cornelius Joseph Jameson."

I reached out my hand to shake his, but he didn't budge.

After a few awkward seconds, Jordyn suggested that we all go inside. The first thing I noticed inside the family home were the pictures on the walls in the living room. Most were of people I didn't know, but I recognized Jordyn's parents from the photo she'd shown me in the car. Jordyn was in a lot of photos, too, but the Jordyn in the photos looked nothing like the Jordyn I knew.

She was as beautiful back then as she was now, yet, there was an innocence about her in the hanging photos. Her eyes were bright and hopeful. Her hair long and flowing down her back versus the edgy curly cut she wore now. In one photo, she looked to be about ten or eleven and stood between her parents as they hugged her, all three of them wearing big smiles. In another, she was having fun with a group of teenage kids around her own age. In a third photo, she was with her grandfather, both making funny faces. Looks wise, she looked a lot like her dad and grandfather, but her facial features were soft like her mother's.

Even though there were a ton of photos of Jordyn smiling, there were a few candid ones that had caught her either looking out of a large living room window, or sitting in her bed reading a book. She looked different in those photos. More reserved. Delicate even. Content.

Anybody worth a damn knew that Jordyn was my type.

Hands down. The woman was a boss. A go-getter. Hell, she was running a successful weed business and yeah, she'd slap me for saying that or referring to her as an organic drug dealer, but that's what I loved about Jordyn. She didn't take any shit from anybody. Me included. How could you not love a woman like that?

Hold the fuck up ... Love? Bruh, did you just say you love her? I shook my head and moved away from the photos. Clearly, all these family photos were fucking with my head. I walked toward the kitchen where Jordyn and Mr. Jameson were already deep in conversation.

"The scholarship banquet is tomorrow," he said, his eyes hopeful. "I'm assuming you're back because you're going?"

Jordyn sighed. "Yes, Grandpa. I'm going to the banquet tomorrow. And before you ask, yeah, I plan on giving the keynote speech ... If they still want me to."

"That's my girl," he said with a huge smile. "I'll make a few calls and let them know that you'll give the keynote. Last I heard, they had a keynote, but I'm sure they'd make room. Everyone in town has missed you."

Mr. Jameson looked from me, back to Jordyn. "Have you told him?"

"Partially," Jordyn said with a shrug.

Mr. Jameson gently squeezed her shoulder. "Then I suggest you make sure he's all caught up by tomorrow. Why don't you two get settled upstairs while I go make those calls?" As he walked out, he stopped when he neared me. "I don't know much about you, young cat, but if my Jordy trusts you enough to bring you home, you can't be all bad." We stood close to the same height, although I had him in weight. His voice lowered so that Jordyn couldn't hear him when he warned, "If you're half of the man that she thinks you are, what she tells you won't change your opinion of her. But if you're like that chump Luther who she used to tell me about, you won't make it back to New York in once piece. I may be an old man, but I still got it and there's not too much I can't do with my cane. Catch my drift, boy?"

"Loud and clear, sir," I replied with a nod. Could I take him if something did go down? Probably. But Mama didn't raise no fool, so the old man had my upmost respect. "I'd never do anything to purposely hurt Jordyn."

He observed me a few seconds more before walking out of the kitchen.

Once we were alone, Jordyn started shuffling from her feet. "How about I make us some coffee and we sit out in the backyard? We have a heated gazebo."

"Sounds good." I didn't want to force her to finish telling me her story, but I'd be lying if I said that I wasn't ready to learn more about Jordyn Jameson.

SEVENTEEN

Jordyn

I STEADIED THE COFFEE CUP IN MY HANDS, WILLING MY fingers not to shake as I led Crayson to the gazebo. Before Crayson had walked into the kitchen, my grandfather was telling me how surprised he was that I'd brought home a man.

It hadn't mattered how many times I told him that we were just friends, my grandpa knew me too well. I *never* let anyone in, so Crayson being in my hometown was saying a lot, and I'd be lying if I said I wasn't grateful he was here.

However, being here also meant that I had to open up to him even more than I'd planned. I wasn't sure why I hadn't thought beforehand that having Crayson attend the scholarship banquet with me meant that I couldn't just tell him about my parents. I had to tell him about the other thing, too.

"This is nice," Crayson remarked, glancing around the

space. The gazebo looked just as I'd remembered it, except instead of my dad's old sofa and recliner chairs, they'd been replaced with outdoor furniture that looked just as comfy, but didn't have the character that my dad's furniture had had.

"Are you cold?"

I glanced up at Crayson who was sitting opposite of me before noticing that now, my entire body was shivering. My nerves were getting the best of me, so just as I'd done when I'd told him about my parents, I decided to rip off the bandage.

"I'm fine." Taking a deep breath, I took a sip of my coffee and relaxed in my chair. "My grandfather wanted me to talk to you because tomorrow, you're going to practically meet the entire town. When you meet them, you'll learn some things about me. Things I'd rather not talk about, but given the circumstances, I know I have to."

I glanced out the window, noticing how clean the backyard looked. My dad used to have a ton of stuff in the yard since he was always checking on his garden or building something for the gazebo. Even though I wasn't looking his way, I could feel his eyes on me. Observing. Waiting.

"I had a good childhood," I told him. "Like I mentioned earlier, my parents were the heart of the community. My mom was an only child, but my grandfather has another son, my Uncle Mike. He's married to my Aunt Lauren and they have three kids. Being such a small family, we were always close. I never got a chance to meet my grandmother or my mom's parents, but Grandpa and I have always been close. Especially after everything." I grew quiet, trying to gather my thoughts and figure out what to say next. "My grandfather didn't always live with us, but he moved in around my eleventh birthday. I was the type of kid that always looked forward to birthdays. Being an only child, my parents used to go all out and I loved being the center of attention. If it were up to me, I would have celebrated my birthday for an entire month. It was the highlight of my life ... until it wasn't anymore."

He studied my eyes, a look of concern that hadn't been there before. I was holding back tears and the fact that I hadn't even told him everything, but was ready to cry like a baby, pissed me off. I was stronger than this. I'd spent years building a tough exterior and overcoming obstacles when faced with adversity. There wasn't much that I couldn't handle, but for some reason, I wasn't handling this conversation the best way I could.

That's because you just need to say it and get it out! I'd replayed the memories of my childhood a million times. I'd thought about everything that had happened to lead me to this point in my life. I'd accepted that everything that had happened had been out of my control, and yet, all of the insecurities I thought I'd overcome, came rushing back as I opened my mouth to tell him my story. To tell him my truth.

"Crayson, I guess what I'm trying to say is that my upbringing wasn't like most people, because instead of going to school dances and hanging out with my friends, I was in and out of the hospital, going through radiation treatments."

His eyes widened as recognition dawned on him. He opened his mouth to say something, but I didn't give him a chance when I pointed out the obvious. "Throughout most of my childhood and adolescence, I battled with a rare form of adolescent leukemia. We caught it late, so treatment was aggressive. I was diagnosed a day before my eleventh birthday and it sucked getting that news on my birthday. Cancer sucks, too, by the way." I tried to lighten the mood even though I'd dropped a heavy bomb. I didn't want his pity, but the look he was giving me was proving that I was getting just that.

———————

Crayson

CANCER? AFTER A FEW MOMENTS, I HAD TO REMIND myself to breathe. I'm not sure what I thought Jordyn had to tell me before the banquet tomorrow, but I hadn't been prepared for the news she'd shared.

"I'm so sorry to hear that," I said. She cringed at my words. "What did I say wrong?"

She waved me off before saying, "Nothing. I just don't want your pity. I've had enough of that to last a lifetime."

"I don't pity you, but I do sympathize with what you've been through." The crease in her forehead relaxed. "How long did you battle the disease?"

She looked out to the backyard again. "In some ways, I feel like I'm still battling with it, but the cancer is gone. Some survivors never like to say that out loud for fear that it will return, but I promised myself I wouldn't be afraid if it did. I'd handle it just like I did before. From age eleven to thirteen and a half, I battled with it. Then it returned at fifteen. I went into remission at eighteen and was given the all's clear at age twenty-three."

"So, you've been healthy for about eight years?" I asked.

She grew quiet, the slight creaks of the gazebo from the chilly wind being blown outside providing the only sound. "Yeah. Besides the occasional cold, I've been good."

Thank God. I hadn't even realized I'd been holding my

breath for her answer. When my breathing returned to normal, I thought more about everything she'd just told me and did some quick math. "You mentioned your parents passed away seven years ago, right?"

Her eyes met mine, the sorrow reflected in the depths hitting me square in my heart. "Yes," she said. "They passed away about nine months after I'd gotten the good news that the cancer was gone." Her eyes got watery, and as much as I wanted to hop out of my chair and pull her into my arms, I knew Jordyn well enough to know that she didn't want that. Not yet anyway. It was hard enough for her to talk to me now, but I felt like she needed to get it out.

"For most of my life, I felt like my parents were holding their breath, waiting for the other shoe to drop. Most of the time, it was because the other shoe did drop, and just when they thought I was getting better, I'd take a turn for the worse." She adjusted herself in her chair and wrapped her arms around her. "Not only did they love community, but they loved adventure. From the time I was diagnosed, my parents stopped vacationing, too afraid to leave me with my grandfather only to receive a call that something bad had happened to me. It took me years to convince them to go on vacation, so once I was clear, they finally listened. They were finally able to take that vacation they'd always dreamed of."

She wiped away a few tears, the light gasp in her voice breaking my heart. Before she even continued with her next words, I'd known what she was going to say. I'd felt her pain. I'd felt her guilt. "They never came back from that vacation that I convinced them to take," she said. "They were touring several different waterfalls in North Carolina, and from what we were told from on-lookers, my father was taking a selfie of them when my mom slipped on a rock. He reached for her and the current took them both under. My mom hit her head and died instantly, but my dad died in a nearby hospital later that day due to complications. I didn't get to say good-bye to either one of them."

I went over to her then, lifting her from her chair and sliding her onto my lap, unable to sit back any longer and not touch her. Comfort her. Let her know that she wasn't in this alone.

"When most kids were playing in the park, I was puking my guts out," she said. "When most teenagers were learning to drive, I was freezing my eggs just in case chemo took an even bigger toll on my body than I was prepared for. For every birthday and every special occasion for about six years, I was sick."

Wiping a few tears from her eyes, I tried my best to offer consoling words. "I hate that you went through all that. Some of us are dealt a shitty hand, and what happened to you and your parents is tragic. I wouldn't wish that kind of pain on my worst enemy. But you're here. You're living. They may not be physically with you, but they are in here." I lightly placed my hand over her heart. "You can tell their story in a way others can't. I'm sure your parents are looking down on you, proud of everything you've accomplished in your life. They raised you right, Jordyn."

She nodded her head. "True, I'm a survivor. I've been beating the odds my entire life. Yet, the moment I'm cleared to start living—and I mean *truly* living—my parents are snatched away from me?" Her voice choked with emotion. "It's not fair, but I told myself at a young age that the world isn't fucking fair. Sometimes, people die. Sometimes, you're the one who dies. The key to getting through all of the shitty parts in life is to know that people can only get close to you if you allow them to. The day after my parents' funeral, I left my home—I left this town—and never looked back. It was easier that way ... to leave a place where everyone either viewed me as the girl with cancer or the girl who'd lost her parents. So, I promised myself one thing and one thing only that day."

I still saw pain and sorrow reflected in her eyes, but she'd pushed those feelings away, replacing them with a determination I hadn't seen all night. "I promised myself that I'd never let anyone get that close to the core of my heart again. Not a friend. Not a family member. Not a lover."

My mouth slightly parted at her admission. She was warning me to stay away from her. She was letting me know that she refused to let someone else in for fear of losing them. She was setting me up for the it's-not-you-it's-me speech I assumed we'd have when we got back to New York. I got the message loud and clear, and for tonight, I'd leave it alone.

However, as I sat there, grateful that she was allowing me to hold her, embrace her, I made a promise of my own and a damn good one. She may have given me fair warning to stay away, but after everything I'd learned about Jordyn, there was no way I was walking away from this. No chance I was letting her go through life pushing people away for fear of losing them.

Through listening to Jordyn's struggle, I realized that what I'd gone through with my ex-wife had to happen to prepare my heart for a woman like Jordyn. I wanted to be her provider. Her lover. Her supporter. Her best friend. If she'd let me, I'd give her *all* of me. I wasn't the possessive type, but she was mine in every sense of the word and I *always* protected what was mine.

EIGHTEEN

Jordyn

To say I was a wreck would be a *HUGE* understatement. Not only was I ready to run out of the nearest exit, but it seemed the entire town had shown up for the scholarship banquet, and if I was a betting woman, I'd assume it was because word had gotten out that I was back in town.

Talking to Crayson last night had been way more emotional than I'd been prepared for—yet, a part of me felt a huge relief with being able to share a part of my life that I kept bottled inside. When we'd gone back into the house, my aunt, uncle, and cousins had all been waiting for us. Once I'd laid eyes on them, I realized how much I'd missed them. We cried. We laughed. We played catch up. Crayson had fit right in, and I didn't miss the eye-winks that my cousin, Angelica, had sent my way every time she caught me watching Crayson talk to my cousins, Isaiah and Steve.

My family was all present at the scholarship banquet, and although I wasn't the keynote, the moderator had asked me to close out the ceremony. The only thing keeping me from freaking out as it neared the end of the event, was listening to Crayson debate with my cousins about sports.

"All I'm saying is that I don't understand why New York Knicks fans are always boosting about the team, when the Knicks have sucked for decades," my cousin, Isaiah, whispered to Crayson.

Crayson waved his hands in disagreement. "Damn son, how many times do I have to tell you that I may live in New York, but I'm not a Knicks fan. LA Lakers all the way, baby."

"Bruh, you ain't hearing me," Steve said. "You wouldn't even be saying this shit if LeBron wasn't on the team. You prolly liked the Cavaliers before the Lakers and Miami Heat before that."

"Nigga, please. I don't follow that dude. Yeah, LeBron is who he is, but I been liked the Lakers."

While they continued to debate which basketball team was the best, I tried to calm my nerves. I must have been too lost in thought, because next thing I know, the moderator drops by the table to tell me I'm up in two minutes.

"Damn," I said after she left. "I'm not ready to do this shit."

Crayson glanced my way and laughed. "My mom would pop me upside my head if I cursed in front of my parents or my aunts and uncles."

"Where do you think I get my potty mouth from?" Jordyn said, pointing to her grandfather. "To get through chemo, instead of reading bedtime stories at nighttime, Grandpa and I used to have screaming matches where we'd yell aloud every curse word we could think of. Tell me, what normal grandfathers do that?"

Grandpa shrugged. "I never claimed to be like these other old geezers. I just wanted my baby girl to release her pain and frustrations out loud. Little did I know, I was turning her into a little cursing sailor."

"Nah Gramps," Crayson said, shaking his head. "She curses more than a sailor. One time, I did something to piss her off and I swear, she yelled a whole paragraph of curse words at me."

The entire table shared a laugh just as they made the announcement for me to come on stage and close the ceremony. My feet felt as if they were weighed down by bricks as I walked to the front of the room, but I needed to do this. I had to speak for my parents.

When I reached the podium, the moderator gave me a quick hug before I greeted the audience. Looking out into the crowd, all I saw were friendly faces. Some I knew. Some I didn't. Yet, there was a calmness that came over me when I said, "First and foremost, as the daughter of James and Stacy Jameson, I would like to thank you for continuing to make sure that my parents' legacy and value of education lives on by offering annual scholarships to these lucky students. It was very hard for me to come here today and speak to all of you, mainly because I can't even begin to explain how much I miss them and how badly I wish they were still alive to see their vision turned into a reality." I looked to Crayson who gave me an encouraging smile. "However, a good friend reminded me yesterday that I can tell their story in ways that no one can. I survived the battle that God placed before me. I wish I'd had more time with them, but I'm here. I'm living. And I want to thank all of you for waiting patiently until I got to this point."

A few neighbors in the audience wiped away their tears. Others intently watched me. I briefly glanced to my grandfather, seeing a source of pride reflected in his eyes. The sight motivated me even more to tell *my* truth. Clearing my throat, I dove into the speech I'd prepared years ago when I thought I would have come back home sooner rather than later. I spoke the words of surviving cancer because I had parents and doctors who refused to give up on me and constantly reminded me that I was strong beyond measure. I shared my parents' love for education and the foundation that one's schooling could offer someone as a platform to better themselves.

I poured my heart and soul into my words, not caring if I cursed a little or my voice cracked, because after years of being away from home, I realized what Crayson said was right. I'd survived. Despite everything, I was still here. My story was one that needed to be told. My parents were people the newcomers of the community needed to hear about.

Standing up there at that podium speaking on behalf of my parents and family did something to me that I hadn't expected or prepared for. It allowed me to release some of the guilt I'd bottled inside. It gave me the opportunity to acknowledge how wrong I'd been for staying away for so long. But I was human. I was allowed to make mistakes. Yet, the key was learning from those mistakes and promising to do better next time.

Speaking to the community did just that. After years of running from my pain and sorrow, I was finally acknowledging that my ordeals had given me deep scars that were carved into my skin in a way that may never fully heal. I was finally growing. *Healing.* And *that* was a beautiful thing.

Crayson

I WAS SO DAMN PROUD OF JORDYN I DIDN'T EVEN KNOW what to do with myself. She'd nailed her speech, and when she'd finished, there hadn't been a dry eye in the building.

Although I wasn't the type to get all emotional and shit, I may have shed a tear or two as I watched my girl shine up on stage. *My girl.* The entire night, the one thing I'd found hard was trying to tell the townspeople exactly what I was to Jordyn. We stuck with the 'good friend' thing, but folks weren't buying it, and by the end of the night, I was claiming her as my girlfriend whether she'd liked it or not. Especially when some stuffy lame looking dude was all up in her space on some "I haven't seen you since high school, do you want to go out sometime and catch up," face-looking ass. I had to shut that shit down real quick because I'd be damned if I'm over here catching feelings and shit while she's out with other dudes reminiscing.

"I still don't understand why you got all Tarzan on me," she said as we walked into the house after returning from the banquet.

"He had some nerve talking to you while I was standing there," I replied. "Besides, he talked like he had a wad of spit in his mouth. Hell, I even seen some spit bubbles at one point. You don't need some dumb ass dude spitting on you while he talks."

She tried to mask her laugh, but I caught her. "I don't know what you mean. I didn't notice anything like that."

My eyebrows rose. "Yeah okay. I bet you were thinking

if he can't hold spit in his mouth, there's no telling what else he *can't* do with his mouth.

At the sound of someone clearing their throat behind me, I turned. *Shit.* I'd forgotten her grandfather was right behind us. "Sorry, sir. I was just saying ..." Hell, I didn't even want to explain it to her grandfather. That shit was just weird.

"I get you," Mr. Jameson said. "That young fella has money, but he is on his third marriage. Word around the streets is that he can't keep a woman satisfied in the bedroom, so as soon as she gets tired of whack ass sex, she slaps him with those divorce papers."

"Grandpa," Jordyn yelled. "Since when did you become the town gossip? Or use the word whack?"

He shrugged. "My girlfriend, Ethel, taught me a thing or two since she's much more hip to y'all young folks talk than I am."

Jordyn crossed her arms and raised an eyebrow. "Hold up, are you dating Ethel who owns the bakery down the street?"

Mr. Jameson smiled with dreamy eyes. "She's my sweetheart, if that's what you mean. She keeps me ... young at heart."

I laughed. "Based off that expression on your face, I bet that's not all she keeps you."

Jordyn slapped my arm. "Crayson, that's nasty."

"That's life." I clasped my hands to my chest. "And your grandfather just became my idol."

Mr. Jameson and I laughed, ignoring Jordyn's groans and claims that we were oversharing.

"I'm staying at Ethel's tonight," Mr. Jameson said. "So you two will have the house to yourselves. And, Jordyn, I want you to check out that, uh, that special room when you get a chance."

He looked at me nervously, although I didn't have a clue why until Jordyn told him, "He knows, Grandpa. Crayson is the owner of the cigar lounge next door that I told you about. The one with the private room that I needed. He knows I own and manage Heavenly Hash."

"Wait a minute." I glanced from Mr. Jameson to Jordyn. "Your grandfather knows about your weed business?"

Mr. Jameson answered before Jordyn got a chance. "Know about it? Hell, who do you think introduced her to it in the first place?" My mouth dropped, blown away by the news he'd just shared.

"Back in the day, my parents didn't believe in medical marijuana," Jordyn explained. "But I was in so much pain all of the time. So my grandpa figured that a little weed couldn't hurt, but we had to get creative. He's a great cook, so he started making me what we called our 'special cookies.' My parents never caught on, and I guess you can say, I got bit by the bug. No one else knows except for my cousin, Angelica. She manages our Maine warehouse along with her husband. They met when I hired him as part of my warehouse staff."

"Get the fuck out of here," I said, placing a hang over my mouth. I turned to Mr. Jameson. "So instead of getting your sons and grandsons into the weed business, you recruited your granddaughters? I've never heard of anything like it."

"It didn't set out to be that way," Mr. Jameson stated. "But my granddaughters are the best business people in the family. JayJay needed someone she could trust, and her and Angelica are close." Mr. Jameson leaned toward Jordyn, but kept his eyes on me. "Damn, you really did tell this young cat a lot, didn't you, Jordy?"

Jordyn blushed. "Sort of. But I trust him. He won't say anything."

Mr. Jameson gave me another one of those looks that spoke wonders. His mouth wasn't moving, but his eyes were saying if I jeopardized Jordyn's business, it was gonna be my ass. Despite his warning, I knew he trusted me a lot more than he had yesterday. While Jordyn had been practicing her speech, Mr. Jameson and I had spoken this morning about my relationship with her. I'd told him what I was feeling and he'd given me some much-needed advice by telling me that, "Jordyn may run away when you tell her you love her, but trust me, she's worth the fight. Be patient with her and she'll come around. She needs someone tough by her side and her last ex was a chump."

By the end of the conversation, I could tell he liked me. He even said I'd reminded him of himself, which I accepted as a compliment. I could see myself being like Mr. Jameson when I got older.

"I'll be on my way then," he said. "Make sure you check on my plants."

"Will do, Grandpa."

Once we were alone, Jordyn walked into my arms. "Thank you for your support tonight."

I brushed her cheek with the back of my hand. "Anytime, beautiful." Leaning down, I captured her lips, suckling on her bottom lip the way I knew she liked. Her hands reached behind me and gave my ass a squeeze, causing me to laugh in between kisses. I'd never thought much of my ass, but every time she got it, Jordyn was pinching it or squeezing it.

As always, our kiss got hotter by the second. She

nibbled on my lip, knowing that I loved that shit. In fact, there wasn't anything she did with her mouth that I didn't love. "I have to check on the trees," she said, breaking our mouths apart. "Follow me."

She didn't have to tell me twice. I followed her into a back room that I hadn't been shown when I'd gotten a tour of the home.

"This is our emergency stash that my grandfather keeps in case something happened to the warehouse we have. It's similar to what I want to have in that private room in New York, but currently keep stored in my spare bedroom."

"This is another world," I remarked, walking through the trees. There was equipment that I'd seen used in the indoor garden my mother had to keep plants warm when it was cold out and a host of other supplies and containers.

"It is."

I stopped looking at the plants and focused all of my attention on Jordyn. She looked so sexy in her sleek navy blue dress, and all night, I'd been thinking about how badly I wanted to take off every stitch of her clothes and make slow, *sweet* love to every part of her body. I was never one that was really into the slow sex thing, but Jordyn's body deserved to be cherished in a way I'd never done with any woman before.

The only problem with my whole slow-sex theory was that Jordyn was sending me nothing but the fuck-me eyes. I watched her slide between the trees, unzipping the back of her dress as she did so. *Damn.* It pooled into a navy puddle at her feet before she stepped out of it, her he̶ ̶licking on the wooden floor as she did so.

"I want to savor you tonight," I said hone

She shook her head. "Devour me."

I shook my head. "Sample you slowly."

She looked around the room, a sexy smirk crossing her lips. "Ever fucked in a room full of weed?"

"Hell nah," I said, stepping closer to her.

"Do you want to fuck me in a room full of weed?"

Do I? Easy. "Hell yeah."

"Good." She met me the rest of the way. "Then I don't want that slow shit. I want it hard. Fast."

She removed her bra, her luscious brown breasts bouncing in front of my face, nipples hard and perky waiting to be lapped up by my tongue. By the time she'd pushed her panties down her creamy coffee thighs, my dick was pressing so hard against my pants, it's a miracle I didn't bust a nut before I even dove inside of her.

"What's it gonna be?" she asked. I surprised her by picking her up and pinning her between me and the wall, careful not to knock over one of the trees. My lips took hers hungrily. I was greedy as hell for her taste. I'd wanted to take my time with her tonight, but it didn't look like that was gonna happen. Slow sex could wait. Tonight, we'd fuck.

NINETEEN

Crayson

"Nice of you to grace us with your presence, princess," Malakai yelled.

I grunted as I walked onto the outdoor basketball court to meet him and Caden who was in town visiting. "It's too damn cold to be out here. Why didn't we just go to the indoor gym up the street?"

"The outdoor court is better," Malakai said, dribbling the ball before tossing it to Caden. "You already know this."

I rubbed my hands up and down my long-sleeved shirt to try to generate more heat. "Fuck that, y'all know I hate the cold. I swear, I'm opening my next cigar lounge in a warm state. This East Coast shit ain't for me."

Malakai looked to Caden, laughter in his tone when he said, "Buddy ass be trippin' like he ain't lived in New York for years."

"Man, quit bitching." Caden tossed the basketball my

way. "In honor of you being a royal pain in our asses, we're gonna play a game of P R I N C E S S instead of one-on-one or H O R S E. You're up first."

I dribbled the ball, wishing I was into the game more than I was. I loved playing ball with my brothers, but a nigga was horny and damn tired of his woman getting calls in the middle of the night from her friend about shit that could wait until the sun came out.

While Caden took his shot, I turned to Malakai. "Bruh, what is with your woman? Jordyn told me she's been taking this wedding shit a little too far. Requests in the middle of the night and day."

He didn't have a chance to respond because we were interrupted by a group of women passing by, making their interest in us known. Malakai continued on with his turn, while Caden looked to me to be his wing man. "Bruh, you ready?"

"Nah, I'm good." I rebounded for Malakai before shooting my shot. It wasn't until I turned around that I realized the ladies were gone and my brothers were staring at me. "What?"

"What do you mean what?" Caden said. "You just turned down flirting with a group of fine ass women. Is it because of Jordyn?"

I shrugged. We hadn't really talked about her, but our friends and my brothers weren't stupid. They knew we were fucking around.

"What's going on with you and Jordyn?" Malakai asked.

I shrugged again. "Nothing much. We chillin'."

"Just chillin'?" Caden laughed.

"Yeah, nigga. That's what I said."

He lifted his chin, his lips twisting in disbelief. "Hell

nah, I don't believe you. If it was something casual, you would have been my wing man just now."

"I'm just not into it," I said. Since I knew they wouldn't let it go, I dropped a little honesty in their direction. "Besides, none of those chicks hold a candle to Jordyn anyway."

"Well I'll be damned." Malakai cupped the ball and walked toward me. "Jordyn has your nose wide open. Have you even messed with another woman since you been hard up on her?"

I shook my head. "I haven't even thought about fucking another woman ever since we shared a kiss on New Year's."

"Damn." Caden's voice carried and echoed off the wall of a nearby building. He looked at me and Malakai. "My brothers up here in New York dropping like flies. Remind me not to sample the pussy in New York because I like my freedom just the way it is."

"Do you love her?" Malakai asked, ignoring Caden. "Do you love Jordyn?"

I looked him dead in the eye, no hesitation when I told him, "Yeah, I love her. But she's gone through a lot, so any time I start talking serious, she changes the subject. She already gave me fair warning not to get serious about her." Grabbing the ball out of Malakai's hands, I took a shot. "She's the one for me, fellas. The only one."

"Love!" Caden yelled. "The one? A mutha fucka like you is in love now? After the way you teased Micah, Malik, and Malakai when they fell in love and found their wives, now you over here talking about the one and shit?"

Malakai turned to Caden. "Bruh, did you and Crayson switch places or some shit? Since when do you get on us about falling in love."

"Not y'all," Caden replied, "this mutha fucka." He

pointed at me, but I didn't care. "Are you serious, Cray? You love her?"

I glanced at Caden and Malakai, the answer leaving my lips easily as I told confirmed, "Yeah, I'm serious. I love her, and as crazy as it sounds, I could see myself marrying her one day. The problem is, she's not ready for a serious relationship. She's not ready for the type of love I'm tryin' to give her."

Malakai turned to Caden and they both shared a knowing look before Caden said, "In that case, brother, you have to convince her to take a chance on love. Whenever I've been around the two of you, y'all are usually fighting like cats and dogs. But I've always thought there was some underlying real feelings involved there. Our brothers may have found their wives, but we can't have these females out here thinking the only Madden men who settle down are these chumps with the M names. We got to let 'em know that the 3C's is outchea, and since Carter is MIA and I don't even have a female worth a damn in my life, you're up, Cray."

Malakai laughed as he looked at his watch. "And while you think about that, we got to get going. We're supposed to meet everyone at Sweet Baby Jay's in an hour, so that's just enough time to get home and shower." Malakai dapped me on my shoulder. "I'm proud of you for not denying your feelings, little brother. Now all you have to do is convince her to take a chance on you. I have faith that you'll persuade her, and I'll even convince my brideszilla wife to calm the fuck down and chill on Jordyn's maid-of-honor duties until you do."

"Thanks, man."

"Anytime." Malakai turned to Caden. "You do know Mama gave her sexiest sons names that start with the letter

M because she's so in love with Dad and his name starts with an M, right?"

"Hell nah," Caden said. "Mama gave her favorite and sexiest sons names that start with the letter C because, let's be forreal, the triplets are her favorites."

Usually I'd be all for this conversation, but I had too much on my mind. I had to persuade the woman I loved to take a chance on me and that shit was *not* gonna be easy.

Jordyn

YOU WOULD THINK AFTER BEING BACK HOME FOR THE first time in years I'd be excited to be back in New York, but that wasn't the case. Crayson and I had already been back for five days and every single one of those days, Avery had looped me into doing something for her wedding. Meaning, I wasn't able to get my freak on like I'd planned on doing after our short trip.

I swear, my ass should have played track in school because a bitch was hopping out of bed every time her phone rang and dashing to the shower, leaving some *very* good dick all alone. Unintended. In her bed. With no warm pussy to keep it company.

It wasn't that I wasn't eager to help my best friend prepare for her big day, but damn, could a girl get a break from all of the wedding shit? It wasn't even my special day, yet, I felt like after all this hard work, I should be walking down the damn aisle, too.

Seriously, bitch? You get some good dick, and already

your ass is ready to say your vows before God and all your close family and friends? The thought almost made me drop the batch of cupcakes I'd taken out of the oven. I'd been having thoughts like that a lot and that shit wasn't good for anybody. I needed to get a grip and get a grip quick!

Glancing at the digital clock on my microwave, I noticed it was time for me to head down to the bar to meet my friends. It paid off having the entire top level to myself, because now that I was down to the last few hundred desserts for the huge order I'd received, I'd needed all the space I could get. Plus, it wasn't a good look for me to have folks at my place right now. If anyone opened one wrong door, they'd probably be high-tailing it out of there and reporting my ass. I couldn't imagine ever giving up my Heavenly Hash business, but I wasn't stupid. I needed to be careful where I stored my shit.

"That smells divine," I said aloud as I sniffed the fluffy cupcakes. Avery and Malakai had decided that we all needed a night out to just chill and not talk about work or their wedding. Granted, meeting at my bar kinda defeated the purpose, but I was cool with it. Unfortunately, their no-wedding-talk meetup had turned into a let's-just-talk-wedding-stuff-the-first-hour-then-chill get together instead.

I let the cupcakes cool, frosted them, and headed down to Sweet Baby Jay's. I knew Crayson's fine ass was already there before I'd even stepped into my bar. There may have been a lot of people at the bar, but I knew Crayson's scent. He always smelled too damn good. The type of good that made you wanna suck his dick all day and let him know how much you worshiped his ass. There was no way I would ever do that shit in real life because dude already had a big ass ego. But I wanted to do it ... Every time I saw his sexy self.

I really need to touch him. The group was all there sitting at our favorite high top table in the corner, but I didn't care how it looked. I greeted Avery, Malakai, Caden, Serenity, and Ty before reaching out to give Crayson a hug. Any excuse for me to bury my face in the crook of his deliciously smelling neck. Just as I'd suspected, he smelled good enough to eat. Took all of my energy not to kiss him behind his earlobe since I knew he liked that shit. When I leaned back up, it was his turn to surprise me as he pulled me back to him, gently bringing my face to his for an appetizing kiss that made my toes curl. His lips were soft. Smooth. We'd kissed so many times before, but this one felt different and I couldn't place my finger on why. I was ready for his tongue before he even dipped it into my mouth, stroking mine the same way he stroked me in the bedroom.

Yeah, we'd seen each other since we'd been back in New York, but we hadn't had much time to talk or even kiss, only ripping off each other's clothes and falling into bed together. My arms went around his shoulders as he pulled me into his opened legs and deepened the kiss. Everyone and anything became background noise as I ignored the chatter around us. This kiss was *everything,* and had he not pulled away, I'm not sure I would have.

"Hey, beautiful," he said, his eyes shining. His smile still sexy as fuck.

"Heyyy." Did my voice sound like a woman in heat? Yeah. Did I give a damn? Abso-fucking-lutely not!

"Earth to Jordyn and Crayson," Ty said. We both turned to face him and our other friends. "If y'all are done mouth-fucking, can we get back to tackling Avery and Malakai's wedding party to-do list? I want to enjoy the rest of the night without brideszilla's crazy ass cracking her whip."

Avery slapped Ty's arm. "Not funny. I'm about to demote you."

"Oh, honey, please demote me," Ty said, rolling his eyes. "I thought being your head bridesmaid in charge would be fun, but you got my black ass running around New York like a bitch on some top-secret mission. And let me tell you, a bitch may look like I work out every day, but these legs weren't made for running."

"Especially the way you sweat," Serenity said with a laugh.

Ty placed his hand over his chest like he was offended. "Girl, I don't sweat. I glisten."

I took a seat at the only open chair across from Crayson. As conversation continued with the items on Avery's list, I tried my best to ignore the way he kept his eyes trained on me, watching my every move. When I took a sip of my cocktail, he observed me. When I adjusted myself in my chair, his eyes found mine. When I laughed at something Ty said, he licked his lips in my direction, which of course only made me think about how much I loved his lips on other parts of my body.

I hadn't known he'd sent me a text until I'd coincidently picked up my phone.

Cray: Am I staying at your place tonight?

I glanced at him before responding.

Jordyn: Of course. I'm already thinking 'bout what we'll do.

He smirked.

Cray: Let me guess. You want to bake together again.

I shook my head.

Jordyn: After that kiss, baking is the last thing on my mind. I'm thinking about #ThatD.

He laughed, but not too loudly.

Cray: Did you really hashtag that! Why are hash-tagging any damn way? Never mind. It's all good. I'm still thinking 'bout #ThatPrettyPussy.

I lifted an eyebrow.

Jordyn: For real? Must be delicious if #Diamond got you kissing me in public, acting brand new and shit.

Now, HE LIFTED AN EYEBROW.

Cray: Girl, you know I've been waitin' to fuck that sweet pussy of yours, so you ain't shocked. #Diamond, huh? Bet. I'll remind #KingCray to whisper some dirty shit to #Diamond tonight.

I GIGGLED, BRIEFLY GLANCING AT HIM.

Jordyn: #KingCray? Lawd, I should have known you would name your dick some bullshit like that.

"DAMN STRAIGHT," HE SAID IN A LOW VOICE.

Cray: This coming from the woman who named her pussy #Diamond.

I NODDED MY HEAD AS I TYPED.

Jordyn: Yeah, I named her. Dudes be

out here naming all types of shit. Case in
point, #KingCray ... Um, #CockyMuch?

HE LOOKED MY WAY, A SLY SMIRK ON HIS FACE.

Cray: Hell yeah, I'm cocky. Grown ass women have been
throwin' their panties at me since I hit puberty.
I have a right to be. And you ain't been complaining
the whole time we've been messing around,
while I've been laying down this pipe on yo' ass.

I SIGHED. I COULDN'T EVEN FAULT THOSE WOMEN
because I saw what they saw. Crayson had a rawness about
him that made me weak-kneed. Even without all his sexy
ass tattoos, he exuded a bad boy vibe. The type of mutha
fucka that your mama warned you to stay away from
because a night with him would end with you being bare-
foot and pregnant. Everything about him looked like great
sex and bad decisions.

Hell, I'd experienced what it felt like to have him inside
of me, so a part of me almost wanted to clap my hands
whenever he walked into a room and thank him for dicking
me down so good. But, there was no way I was pumping up
his ego that damn much. A bitch had to keep some form
of class.

Jordyn: Rumor has it, you ain't the most well-endowed

Madden brother. From my experience,
you lay it down okay ...
But I hear there's better out there.
#MaybeI'mFuckinWitTheWrongBrother

To prove my point, I shot googly eyes Caden's way since I didn't want him thinking I was referring to Malakai and was a home wrecker who would ever go after my best friend's man.

By the time I looked back at Crayson, his pupils were dilated and his jaw was clenched. I laughed because he had to know I was bluffing. I wasn't interested in Caden, but men tended to get jealous even if they didn't need to be. To fuck with him even more, I shot another quick text.

Jordyn: I mean, y'all do look the same. But he's more
country
and my mama used to always tell me that
she wanted me to settle down with a nice country boy.

That part was true, my mama did always used to tell me that. She grew up in the south, so even though my dad was all city, she'd always said she saw me with someone southern. *Oh, Mama, that is sooooo not my type.* My type was sitting right across from me, looking like he was ready to punch a hole in the table. Or fuck me on the table. One of those. Crayson may have grown up in Arkansas, but he was a city boy, all day every day.

He raised an eyebrow, clearly not liking the game I was playing. Little did he know, I was all about #KingCray right now, so even though he didn't like what I was texting, I couldn't lie, it was fun getting a rise out of him.

After a few seconds, his scowl was replaced by another one of his sexy smirks.

Cray: The next time I hit that and you're on your sixth orgasm, I want you to remember why I fucked you so good. When I squeeze and bite your juicy ass, remember that no one can worship that shit like me.

Next time we fuck, I want you to think about these texts as I suck your clit and lick your delicious pussy. Jordyn, I don't share with nobody, and in case I wasn't clear when we first started this shit, I claimed you then and I claimed that pussy. You're mine in every sense of the word.

I GLANCED HIS WAY AND CAUGHT HIS EYES, HIS WORDS in the text messages making me hornier than I'd ever been. I should be cursing his ass out. I needed to remind him that nobody could stake a claim on me. I never used to be one for crass words, but damned if Crayson's matter-of-fact way of talking didn't get me all hot and bothered. Dude had me squirming in my seat, already jotting down my sins in my mind since a bitch would have to go to church to repent every day this week for everything he'd just texted.

My pussy ached just thinking about what he was about to do to me later. I was so busy trying to calm a pulsing Diamond to stop her from causing a damn scene in front of our friends, that I didn't even know he'd sent the last text until I glanced back at my phone.

> Cray: Next time we fuck, when you're screaming my name and moaning 'til your throat is dry, I want you to think about this moment. Think about the exact instant when you knew you'd fucked up.

AND JUST LIKE THAT, MY PANTIES WERE EVEN MORE soaked.

TWENTY

Crayson

It took a couple hours for us to wrap up with our friends, but as soon as we did, Jordyn and I walked over to my cigar lounge since I hadn't been able to show her the door I'd finished for the private room in the basement.

"It's perfect," she exclaimed, toting a container in her hand. "I love how discreet it looks." If you didn't know the metal door was there, you'd never be able to tell with the way I'd designed it to blend in with the metal shelves I'd installed.

"Thanks." I led her into the private space, her eyes lighting up as she talked about all of the product she could store in there. She was even more excited when I showed her the climate control monitor I'd mounted and the padding I'd installed to part of the floors for extra cushion.

"You're amazing," she said.

"So amazing that you'll finally tell me what's in that container you're holding?" I asked.

She raised her chin. "Yeah, but not yet."

I shook my head as I walked her back upstairs, channeling all of the patience I had so that I wouldn't jump her right there in the basement. All those messages we'd sent each other had me ready to throw her over my shoulder and fuck her senseless, but first, I wanted her to see the rest of the updates since Undefined Sanctum opened in a couple weekends.

My comfortable mahogany leather chairs and circular glass tables had finally arrived and were paired with massive coffee-colored couches in the lounge area. Instead of the typical black, circular bar stools, I'd gone with high leather chairs that were the same as the ones at my high tables.

"It's exactly how I would imagine the good ole' boys club looking back in the eighties, only with a modern twist."

"That's exactly the look I was going for. Even the design for both bars is consistent with the overall deep and dark décor. I plan on keeping the lighting dimmed and low, and will even have entertainment here from time to time. And check this out ..." I walked over to my cigar showcase. "This is where I'll display my top cigars, and right through those closed doors is my cigar shop."

"I love it," she said, admiring the glass showcase before running her fingers over my brown and gold granite countertops. "Did you do anything different with the private cigar suites?"

"Nah, they were finished first, so you saw all of the updates for those during Malakai and Avery's engagement party. But I did finish a special spot that I want to show you."

She smiled. "Lead the way."

Walking to the back of my lounge, I led her past the private suites and through a set of locked double doors to my latest project and the one that had kept me up most the past couple of days with final touches.

"Originally, I was going to use this large space for storage. But upon discovering there was much more to this room than what meets the eye, I found a better use for it instead." Taking out my keys, I turned to Jordyn who was anxiously waiting to see what was on the other side of the door.

Instead of explaining to her what she was about to see, I figured it was best to let her experience it for herself. I unlocked the door, clicked on the light, and motioned for her to step inside. The moment she did, she gasped and placed the container she was holding on the coffee table.

"This is beautiful," she said, doing a three-sixty in the room. "I've never seen anything like it." Her eyes went to the living space first, as she took in the plush burgundy furniture and mini bar in the corner. Next, she walked over to the kitchenette, opening the stocked mini-fridge and cigar stand.

"All of those cigars are dessert themed," I said. "They remind me of you, so I keep them in here. And that smaller appliance right next to the fridge is a chilled dessert holder. It will keep cupcakes, cookies, and anything else you bake fresh until we're ready to eat them."

She turned to me and lifted an eyebrow. "Did you install this for me to enjoy?"

"I did. I figured you could store some of your *special* desserts here for us to enjoy so you're not always running up to your apartment," I clarified. "But this next section is one we can both enjoy together." I opened the door to our right, revealing a large king-sized bed that sat to the right of the bedroom, and a jacuzzi to the left.

"Holy shit." Her hands flew to her mouth as she walked deeper into the room and noticed that there was also a full bathroom and standing shower connected to the bedroom. "It's like a private haven equipped with everything you'd need to relax ... away from life's distractions." She looked to the bed again. "And preferably naked."

I chuckled. "I like the way you think. For my staff that I'm training, I told them this section is my private quarters and strictly off limits. But between me and you, I'm calling it CJ's Oasis."

She laughed. "What does the CJ stand for?"

I gave her a sheepish grin. "Crayson and Jordyn. I created this space for us. We're always so busy with work at my cigar lounge or your bar, and since you mainly use your apartment for Heavenly Hash, I figured it would be nice for us to have a place to escape that's close to our businesses in case we need to check in."

She looked at me, her eyes wide in astonishment as she stammered, "Y-you created this with m-me in mind?"

"I did." I took a step closer to her. "I know we never talked about it, but to me, you and I are in a relationship. And I'm not talking about a fuck buddies kinda thing. I'm talking about a committed relationship in which we date with the intention of being together for a long time." She looked at me in shock, taken aback by my words, so I figured I had to lay it all out there in case I didn't get a chance.

"Ever since we kissed on New Year's, I haven't been with anyone else. Hell, I haven't even thought about being with anyone else because the only woman I want to be with is you." I took a few more steps toward her and let my words sink in. "Jordyn, you have been through hell and back, yet you've managed to overcome every obstacle life has thrown your way. And on top of all of it, you also own and manage a bar and Heavenly Hash. I have never met a woman like you before, and even more important, I've never felt like I can be myself and be accepted by a woman, faults and all. I'm an asshole sometimes and that probably won't change, but when it comes to people I care about, they get the best parts of me if they're willing to look beyond the surface at who I really am."

I took a deep breath, grateful that she let me pull her into my arms since she was still looking shocked as hell by my words. "I'm not trying to make some long, sappy speech about how much you mean to me, because you won't respond to that. I'm not gonna tell you how much I admire the woman you are and value your determination, because you don't need my validation. Your grandfather even told me that you visit cancer patients every week so they know they aren't alone. So I won't remind you that you truly have a heart of gold, because I know you don't want me to be impressed by that." My eyes dropped to her lips. "I'm not even gonna get into the fact that as corny as it sounds, my breath catches when you walk into a room because you're drop dead gorgeous and embody such a raw sexiness, I can't help but stare at you sometimes."

I placed a brief kiss on her lips, unable to help myself. "And lastly, I won't even bore you by telling you that you, Jordyn Jameson, have my mind, body, and soul so wrapped up in you, that I'll be damned if I ever let you go so another man can make you his. So you may not be ready to hear this, but I love the hell out of you, and although you don't need to say it back, you need to know that I don't plan on going any damn where."

Her mouth parted at my words, so I did the only thing I

could think of doing to stop her from over-thinking what I'd just said ... I gently placed my hand on the back of her head, pulled her toward me, and kissed her.

———

Jordyn

HE LOVES ME. CRAYSON MADDEN LOVES ME. IT WASN'T the first time that a man had said he loved me, but damn, I hadn't seen it coming. If I were being honest with myself, I'd know that it was the first time I *truly* wanted another man to say those words. I mean, I guess a part of me knew that he had strong feelings for me, but I hadn't been prepared for the night to go the way it was.

My insides were twisting into a bundle of nerves, and even with his lips on mine, it couldn't stop my brain from overthinking. Once my thoughts started talking way too fast for me to keep up, I broke our kiss and walked back into the living area of the space.

Crayson didn't follow me, so I grabbed my container and walked back into the bedroom. The expression on his face was a mixture of relief that I didn't leave and uncertainty that he'd laid out too many of his feelings. He was right, I wasn't ready to say *I love you*, but it wasn't because I didn't share the same feelings. It was because once I said those words, I couldn't take them back. Once they were out in the universe, *once he knew how I truly felt about him,* that meant he was locked into that part of my heart that currently had a do-not-fuck-with-a-bitch-unless-you-want-to-get-cut sign hanging off it.

It wasn't that I didn't want to fall in love. The problem was that I didn't want the all-consuming kind of love. The kind that made you lose your damn mind. And Crayson with his bad-boy vibe, smooth, brown skin, tattooed arm sleeve, and deep amber eyes was definitely that type.

But it doesn't matter, girl, you already fell for him. I knew I was already in love just as surely as I knew there was no running from it. But I had to let his words marinate in my mind, so in the meantime, I wanted to show him what I'd been cooking up. He wasn't the only one full of surprises.

"They're for you." I opened the container and handed it to him. "I made dessert cigars, or cigar edibles, whatever you want to call them. And I made sure I made them taste like an actual cigar, but, I added my special ingredient."

He took them out of the container. "They look and smell amazing. And I have the perfect flavored cigar to pair with it."

I quirked my eyebrow. "Are you suggesting we get high and smoke cigars?"

His lips curled to the side in a slow smile, his one dimple winking at me, daring me to say his idea wasn't a great one. "That's exactly what I'm suggesting."

Instead of responding, I walked back into the living area and placed both cigar edibles on a couple napkins I'd spotted when I'd walked into the room. The couch was looking mighty comfortable, so I took a seat Indian-style, while Crayson went to the cigar stand and returned with a kit.

He opened the Maplewood box, the delicious scent immediately wafting through my nostrils. "Wow, it smells good," I said. "Better than my dessert."

"Hell nah," he shook his head, "nothing smells better

than your dessert. But I guess this is a close second." He picked up one of the cigars, bringing it to his nose. "This cigar is called The Ashton Aged Maduro, and I only recently grew a fascination for the taste last year."

I watched as his fingers ran over the cigar, hypnotized by his movements.

"You touch it like it's delicate," I remarked.

"That's because it is delicate." His eyes held mine for a brief second before going back to the cigar. "You see, cigars are a lot like women. The good ones—the flavorful ones— are always the hardest to find. And it's not because they don't exist. It's because it takes a special kind of person to find them. Savor them. Share their love for them with others." He ran the cigar under his nose. "This one is a medium spice with bursts of chocolate and coffee flavor. The moment it touches your lips, you can't help but relish in its natural sweetness. Remind you of anything?" He wiggled his eyebrows, sending me into a laughing fit. I was laughing so hard I could barely speak.

"You did not just compare women to cigars."

"I did, and you liked it." He handed me the cigar and reached up to light it.

"Wait," I said, catching him before he did so. "You have to try the edible I made first so you can taste the cigar flavor."

I passed him his dessert and he took a huge bite, his eyes lighting in delight. "Damn, this shit is good as hell." He took another bite. "And it does taste like a cigar. The flavor shouldn't work, but it does."

"I know." I leaned back onto the couch, smiling hard as hell before taking a bite of my own dessert. We ate in silence, our eyes focused on one another, each observing the other's behavior. *You should tell him how you feel. He opened up to you, so you should do the same.*

"I like you," I said, fidgeting with the edge of my napkin. "And I guess by like, I mean really, *really* care deeply for you in a way that I never have any man before. But I ... I'm scared." I meet his eyes. "I'm scared that caring for you the way that I do will ruin me."

Crayson shook his head. "I'd never do anything to hurt you."

"Not on purpose," I replied. "But sometimes, things happen that are out of our control, and I'm the type of person who doesn't know how to half-ass anything. When I care about someone, I care with my *entire* heart. So, while I may have extremely strong feelings for you, I need to take things slow. And by slow, I mean oh-my-god-watching-molasses-dry-is-quicker-than-this kinda thing."

He leaned closer to me, a twinkle in his eye. "First you give up that pussy, then you ask me to take things slow?"

I slapped him on his shoulder. "I don't mean in the sexual department. I'm talking about emotions and all that relationship stuff."

"I know what you mean," he said with a laugh. "And I'm willing to go at whatever pace you want to set as long as we agree to be monogamous and you promise to never push me away because you're scared, but rather, let me in on how you're feeling."

"Deal," I told him, reaching out my hand to shake on it. He laughed, but he shook my hand, and in some ways, I truly did feel like we were signing a binding contract because lord knew, I was hooked on Crayson and even though I talked a mean game, I wasn't going anywhere.

Our hands lingered together for a little while, one of his

tattoos catching my eye. "I meant to tell you ... I love what your tattoo says."

He glanced at his arm. "Life will feed the truth." We disconnected our hands and he touched the tattoo. "It was actually one of the first tattoos I got right after I'd decided that I was sick of getting arrested and didn't want to get caught in the system. To me, it means that life may throw you curveballs that you don't see coming, but through your struggles, through the decisions you make in life, your truth will come as a result. Now, whether you have to search for that truth, or you recognize it for what it is, depends on the individual. I acknowledged mine and I decided to change my life around and stop rolling the dice, hoping I get lucky and not get caught doing something stupid. Every day, I live my truth. No other way to be in my eyes."

I nodded my head, agreeing with everything he'd just said, but being too amazed by his words to respond. Crayson was always surprising me when I least expected it, and the crazy thing was, the parts of him that used to drive me crazy, were now the ones forcing me to take an even deeper look at him.

After we'd finished the dessert, Crayson lit our cigars. I'd smoked a cigar before, but the moment I took my first puff, I noticed what Crayson was talking about. Instead of the aftertaste that usually made me scrunch my face in dislike, I moaned at the sweet flavors on my tongue.

"Okay, so maybe you're right." I took a couple more puffs. "That flavor is bomb."

"Told you." He took a few puffs of his cigar. "You're gonna learn that I'm always right."

"Ha! Never."

Conversation flowed as we smoked our cigars and talked about things we hadn't discussed with each other yet. Yeah, we bickered—because, after all, we were still Jordyn and Crayson—but there was a level of understanding and comfortability that hadn't been there before. The air was still lit with sexual tension, but we were content with talking and not rushing to rip each other's clothes off.

Halfway through our conversation, Crayson interrupted me when he said, "Just a reminder, you don't have to say the words until you're ready. Until you truly feel them in your heart."

I knew what he was talking about because the truth was, I was already feeling it. Hell, I was swimming in it, but I wasn't ready to say it and that was okay. Crayson was teaching me how to let myself off the hook and not stress out as much about things I couldn't control. He was different. I was different. *We* were different.

TWENTY-ONE

Two weeks later ...

Crayson

"Here's to the man of the hour," Malakai said, raising his glass for a toast. "I'm proud of you, brother. May your business continue to grow and prosper." Similar sentiments were expressed from others as we stood near the bar in Undefined Sanctum while the DJ prepared to play some nineties hits at Jordyn's request.

"Thanks, man." I met his glass, toasting with others who were standing around our small group as well. Tonight, was the second day of the grand opening weekend for Undefined Sanctum, and so far, all signs pointed to this cigar lounge being one of my most popular ones yet. The elite membership program I'd initiated was already at capacity, so my PR and marketing team were already working on new concepts to create different membership tiers, but maintain the exclusivity.

Jordyn's businesses were doing great, too—with Sweet Baby Jay's being named one of Brooklyn's top bars, and Heavenly Hash fulfilling the large edible order she'd gotten and completing two smaller orders just last week. My baby was doin' the damn thang and I couldn't be prouder.

The only thing that would make my night that much better was if I could find wherever her sexy ass went. She'd missed Malakai's toast, and come to think of it, I hadn't seen her in a half hour.

Just when I was about to ask Avery if she knew where Jordyn was, my phone pinged with a text message from her.

I'm in CJ's Oasis ... waiting for you.
Don't make me wait long.

"You ain't said nothing but a word," I whispered to myself, slipping my phone back into my pocket.

"Uh, thanks for stopping coming," I said to our group of friends. "I'll catch y'all later."

Serenity smacked her lips. "In other words, you and Jordyn can't keep your hands off each other."

"And y'all about to go do the nasty," Ty added.

"Man, in the middle of your grand opening?" Malakai asked, motioning around the room.

"Bruh, I know you ain't talking with all that sex you and Avery be having in the conference room in your office suite."

"Eww." Ty scrunched up his nose. "Y'all be gettin'

freaky in the same place we have our weekly meetings? Aww, nah."

Serenity shook a finger at them. "That shit ain't right."

Malakai's eyes got big and looked at Avery before glancing at my retreating back. "Damn, you didn't even have to put me out there like that."

"You started that shit. Bye, mutha fucka." I waved my hand behind me, refusing to slow my steps. I passed by several employees on my way to the Oasis, but I didn't have time to see if they needed anything, nor did I care if they knew what I was up to. This was my damn day, so I deserved to be rewarded.

Using my key, I unlocked the door, my mouth dropping open when a very naked Jordyn stood in the middle of the room wearing nothing but those fuck-me black heels that I loved.

"You look so fucking good," I told her, right before I lifted her Tarzan-style, damn near running to the bedroom before tossing her onto the bed.

She laughed. "Eager much?"

"For you? Always." I started removing my clothes, ignoring the fact that I could hear commotion down the hallway coming from the private suites.

"Is the noise bothering you?" she asked.

I shook my head. "Hell nah. You?"

She bit her bottom lip. "I know we won't make a habit of fucking during business hours, but I kinda like the idea of somebody hearing us. Betta yet, hearing how loudly I moan when you slide your dick inside of me."

"Fuck." She was my perfect match. I almost came on the spot. Being around Jordyn tended to do that to me. She was my future. I wanted to marry this woman, which meant, I would have to get a grip because no woman wanted a man who busted one before she did. I'd never get mine before she got hers. Point blank, period.

Once I was completely naked, I leaned down toward her, but she stopped me and pushed me up against the wall instead.

"What are you ..." My voice trailed off the moment she dropped into a squat position, glistening pussy on full display. Without warning, her soft lips wrapped around my dick, her warm tongue making me brace myself against the useless wall.

"Fuck. Fuck. Fuck." The object was *not* to come too fast, but the way Jordyn was moving her damn mouth, I wasn't even sure I could last two minutes.

"Baby, if you keep that up, this will be over much too fast."

She glanced up at me, her eyes sneaky as hell while her tongue continued to get to work. She wasn't gonna let up, meaning, I could either stand there and enjoy it, or use all of the strength I had to pull my dick from her sexy mouth.

I was on the brink, my thighs tensing up as I prepared myself to come like I knew I would, when she plopped me out her mouth. I looked down at her in confusion, until I noticed her eyes get watery before she told me, "I love you, Crayson. I love you more than you'll ever realize, and I want to thank you for loving me without restriction ... without limitations. I guess, just thank you, baby. Because of you, I realized that life may be shitty at times, but getting through it with someone by your side is a better way to live."

With a sly smile, she went right back to sucking my dick, the quick move really fucking with my state of mind. Remember that strength I was searching for moments earlier? Her words, her *beautiful* fucking words, gave me the strength to lift her up and pin her back onto the bed.

Looking down at her, I reminded myself that I was one lucky bastard to have won the love of Jordyn Jameson. Even so, I just had to point out that, "Only you would choose the moment when you have my dick in your mouth to tell me that you love me."

She giggled. "It seemed like the right time. It's not just about the sex with us, but damned if we don't connect on a whole other level when we fuck."

"You damn right," I said, just before I proved my point by diving into her sweet center in one long stroke. "How long will it take before you're ready for me to propose?"

"What the hell?" she asked breathlessly. "I just said I love you, and you already want to get married?"

I smirked. "When you know, you know."

"This better not be a proposal."

"Nah, when it happens, you won't see it coming." *Although the more I think about it, I did tell my brothers when I proposed, it was gonna be some place warm.* I buried my dick even deeper inside of her. *Nah, bruh. This ain't the type of warmth you were talking about. Close to it though.*

Leaning down, I popped one of her nipples into my mouth, enjoying the sweet scent of whatever lotion she'd put on that combined with a scent that was all uniquely Jordyn. *I could bottle up her smell and drink a glass of this shit.* Yeah, I said it. Some folks may say that was some freaky ass shit to bottle up someone's juices and drink it like I would some damn water, but I was a freaky mutha fucka and I never claimed to be anything else.

I hadn't been ashamed of how much I'd wanted Jordyn when I first met her, so I damn sure wasn't ashamed by how much I still and *always* would want her. I took her right leg and pushed it high above her shoulders, her foot tapping the headboard with each stroke.

"Damn, Crayson." She moaned cursed words into my ear, true to her style, and I liked the shit out of it. Pleasing her would always be my main priority and the position let me dive deeper into her wetness, bringing her even closer to her orgasm. When her soft moans turned to yelling, I switched our positions once again, twisting her onto her side and making my strokes flow into a slow and steady rhythm. I'd been doing that a lot lately ... making sweet love to Jordyn by pouring all of my emotion into my strokes. How she managed to dip out her tongue and lick along my tattoos in her current position, I'd never know, but she did and the warm wetness made me sit in her pussy for a while and just enjoy how it felt to be enclosed by her sweetness.

This was the feeling I'd been thinking about all night. *This* was the reason I'd move mountains and rivers to be by this woman's side supporting her in every way I knew how. It wasn't just that her pussy was so good—and trust me, that shit was amazing—but it was also the fact that this woman accepted me. All of me. And I accepted her, too. We worked because we saw the good in each other and accepted our faults for what they were. I loved the shit out of this woman and she loved the shit out of me.

I looked down at our bodies, connecting in ways most folks only saw in porn. This was my woman. *She* was my future. I hadn't just claimed her. She'd claimed me. And when she rolled her waist and pumped her hips to meet my strokes the way that she was doing now, it reminded me that life could be perfect, everything could be perfect ... as long as you met someone who complemented your kind of crazy.

BONUS SCENE

(Because friends don't let friends get high alone)

One month later ...

Jordyn

"So, what you're saying is, you're a boss bitch."

I laughed at Avery's comment since she'd been repeating the same line for the past twenty minutes. When Avery and Malakai had popped up to my apartment unannounced and late as hell on a freaking Sunday babbling about more wedding stuff, I'd had enough. I'd shot Crayson one look of annoyance and we both knew what we needed to do.

I didn't want to tell all of our friends, but Avery and Malakai needed some edibles in their life. Why? Because they were too damn high-strung about their wedding. Crayson swore it was because Malakai was kind of a big deal in the creative world, but my gut was telling me Avery would have been a bridezilla regardless. *It's always the nice ones.*

"My friend is a boss bitch," Avery muttered again.

I sighed. "How many times are you gonna say that?"

"As many times as it takes to sink in," she replied.

Malakai groaned. "That may take a while."

"This rug feels so good," Crayson said.

I laughed. "That's just the edibles kicking in."

After I'd given Avery and Malakai a brief run-down of Heavenly Hash, they'd been more than eager to try some of my edibles. I hadn't told them everything because let's face it, Crayson and I weren't cut from the same cloth as them whether we admitted it to ourselves or not. Avery and Malakai were ... Well, Avery and Malakai.

Besides, I liked Crayson being the only one to know everything about me inside and out. Especially if his ass was going to propose and officially make me a Madden like he insisted on reminding me any chance he got. A bitch was still in shock that he was so ready for marriage, but deep down, I was elated as hell. I already felt like I was his, but I wouldn't mind a nice rock to make it official.

"I'm with Crayson," Malakai said. "This rug is niceeeeee."

I shook my head, secretly loving how funny my friends were when they were high. I'd convinced all three of them to join me on the floor, and now, these fools were all looking to the ceiling, lost in their own candy land worlds, and judging by the way I felt like I was levitating in the air, I'd say I was starting to feel it, too.

"My mind is blown," Avery remarked as she moved her hands to emphasize her point.

"Do that again," Malakai said, wearing a goofy smile.

"My mind is blown." This time, she waved her hands even more and we all ohhh'd and ahhh'd about absolutely nothing, but to us, it looked like her hands were moving twice as fast as they were.

"What chu thinkin' bout', baby'?" Crayson asked.

"Shit. You?"

He smirked. "That pussy."

"Dumbass." I swatted toward his head, but he ducked, causing me to hit Avery.

"Oh shit," she said in a panic. "The ceiling is collapsing."

"No, it's not." Malakai pulled her to him. "Jordyn hit you by accident."

She settled down, but didn't look convinced as she continued to observe the ceiling as if it would fall any moment. When she finally did relax, Avery picked up right where she left off. "Wow, my friend is dope."

I smiled. "You're dope, too, boo."

"But you're like a boss ass bitch because you run shit, right?"

"Yep."

She lifted her hand. "You're a give-me-your-money-fool-before-you-get-my-product kinda bitch." She'd even deepened her voice on that one.

Squinting my eyes, I glanced at a confused Crayson. "Uh, no," I said. "I make edibles, Avery, I'm not on the corners selling weed."

"I feel you, sis," she said. "You got to keep that shit on the hush, hush. I got you."

Crayson held his stomach as he laughed. "Tomorrow, you have to re-tell her everything you mentioned tonight because these edibles got her trippin'."

"Who the hell made up the term trippin' anyway?" I

asked. "Like, do y'all think a group of people were laying around like us and were like 'that's a catchy phrase, let's say that shit and see if it catches on'?"

"I know, right," Avery exclaimed. "Maybe someone tripped and someone said 'why you always trippin' in a literal sense and the shit stuck."

"I like Avery's explanation better," Malakai said.

Crayson snorted. "Of course you're siding with your soon-to-be-wife despite her lame reason."

"Hey, not cool." Avery pushed Crayson on the shoulder.

"You're right, baby," I said. "This rug feels so damn good." I spread my arms and legs as if I were making a snow angel, enjoying the plush fabric on my back. Soon, the others were doing the same thing, although the guys were trying to be more discreet with it.

"Can we get high like this every day?" Avery asked, clapping her hands together in excitement.

I shook my head. "Uh, no, we can't. But maybe once a month?"

"Consider it a deal." She squealed. "Wait, how do you spell consider?"

"P U S S Y," Crayson replied.

I frowned. "That's not how you spell it."

"I know," Crayson said, nodding his head. "I spelled pussy because I'm wondering when we'll get to that part."

I turned to Crayson. "Is that all men think about? When they gettin' some?"

"Hell yeah." Crayson laughed. "Getting high makes you horny as fuck, but Malakai and I are trying to behave."

"Amen, brother." Malakai dapped Crayson's fist.

I looked around the circle until my eyes caught Avery's. I instantly knew we both had the same idea.

Without warning, I straddled Crayson, placing my lips on his slowly, deliriously. I didn't even know when Avery and Malakai stood up, until I briefly looked to my front door and saw Malakai kissing Avery's neck while she pointed to me and said, "That's my bitch. That's my boss bitch."

I laughed, as I told her to get back to her old place, before glancing back down at the amazing man lying beneath me. The man who loved to piss me off and apologize by making love to me to the point where I couldn't even think straight. The man who wasn't afraid of my secondary lifestyle, but instead, embraced my business and was now one of my partners in crime. Case in point. This current moment. Right now. On my nice ass rug with my bomb ass friends.

"What are you thinking about?" he asked.

"How much I love you."

He smirked. "That's funny, because I was thinking about how much I want to fuck you, boss bitch."

"You're such an asshole. I was tryin' to be sweet."

"Baby, you'd walk all over my ass if I wasn't one."

I shook my head no, when really I meant *yeah*. I heard noise in the hallway and my mind went back to Avery. "I know I promised her we'd do this every month, but I may never give that girl an edible again. She talks a mile a minute when she's high."

"I heard that," Avery yelled through my closed front door. I got off Crayson and opened my door to find Avery and Malakai hadn't gotten that far. Avery still had a key to her old apartment, but apparently, they couldn't even make it down the damn hallway.

"Why are y'all on the floor?"

Malakai looked guilty as hell, but he choose to ignore my question and instead said, "There's no bed or furniture in Avery's old place anymore and I can't drive. Can we crash in your spare bedroom?"

I looked at Crayson and we both laughed. "Yeah, you can." I helped them up and led them to the spare that was usually off limits. "But y'all have to promise me that you won't touch anything, okay?"

Avery scrunched her eyes together. "What would we touch?"

I opened the door, and before I could even get the words out, Avery was running into the room yelling, "Oh my God, baby, it's a weed tree. She got a whole tree. Not a half tree. A big dumb ass tree. Can I get one? Please, baby, pretty please?"

I shut the door on her loud ass, grateful that no one was located on my floor to hear her screaming about the damn tree. "She's a mess, right?" I asked Crayson who was making his way toward me.

Instead of responding, he pulled me to him, and kissed me in that same way that made my toes curl. By the time we made it to my bedroom, I was already stripping off my clothes, hoping that we didn't disturb our friends because, baby, sex with Crayson was always amazing as hell. But sex with Crayson when we were high as fuck was on another level entirely.

THE END

WOULD LOVE TO HEAR FROM YOU!

I hope you enjoyed #ClaimedByCrayson! I love to hear from readers! Thanks in advance for any reviews, messages or emails :). Keep turning for more goodies!

Also, stop by my online Coffee Corner and get the latest info on my books, contests, events and more!

www.bit.ly/SherelleGreensCoffeeCorner

Save and Author! Leave a Review!

#BLESSEDBYMALAKAI

Every man has his weakness. For prominent painter and sculptor Malakai Madden, that weakness has always been women. Now, he's finally ready to settle down and shower one woman with his love. There's just one major problem. Overnight, he's gained thousands of Twitter followers after his obsessive ex decides to leak some private information. To make matters worse, a well-known media source retweets them! Suddenly, every woman wants a piece of Malakai. And when the #BlessedByMalakai hashtag starts trending, he's dodging women left and right, and blocking his crotch like he's secret service securing the president. If he's ever going to get his life back and find his future wife, he needs to solve this problem and he needs to solve it fast!

Image consultant Avery Nightingale can't believe she's landed a meeting with a huge potential client. She knows all about the #BlessedByMalakai hashtag and she's ready to pitch her ideas. However, when she meets the man behind the Twitter legend, she's rendered speechless and Mr. Make You Moan is not impressed. He agrees to hire her on one condition. Avery must promise not to feed into the social media craze as others have failed to accomplish before her. She agrees. After all, it's just one rule, right?

Check out an excerpt on the next page

MALAKAI

I'm no gentleman. Never have been. Granted, if you asked the people who know me best, they would say that I hold open doors for women, I respect my elders, I donate to several charities, and I'm always there for the people I love. But make no mistake. I'm no gentleman. At least not in the bedroom.

I'd never apologize for my desire to fulfill a woman's needs and fantasies by making every intimate moment we share better than the last. And until today, I'd never questioned my sexual escapades. Up until today, I'd never thought twice about leaving a woman so satisfied, she couldn't help but boast about me to her friends. Up until today, I would have sworn that there was nothing wrong with a woman feeling like a night with me meant unlimited orgasms *guaranteed*.

Too bad that today, the unthinkable happened. Today, with each passing minute, I was regretting the fact that I was so good at what I do. I loved women. I appreciated women. But in this moment, I'd do anything to change my past actions and re-evaluate the steps I took that landed me in my current predicament.

Run faster, I thought to myself, taking longer strides and trying my best to block out all of the voices yelling behind me.

"Malakai Madden, you're a sex god!"

"Malakai Madden, I want to have your babies."

"Oh my God, Malakai, I want to be blessed by you."

The last comment made me turn around and face the mob of women who were currently chasing after me on one of the busiest streets in downtown Chicago.

"Ladies, this is a bit much. Don't you think?" I yelled behind me. In the wave of "no's" that echoed through the crowd, I heard a voice I recognized. The voice of the woman who started this crazy mess in the first place.

"Malakai, choose me," Roxanne yelled over the women. "Marry me. Love me. You know we're perfect together."

I shook my head as I picked up speed and prayed that Bare Sophistication, the lingerie boutique my cousin's owned, was open considering it was so early in the morning. Out of the corner of my eye, I caught two police officers on a side street directing morning traffic.

"I'm so glad to see you fellas," I called, approaching the police officers. "A crazy mob of women has been chasing me for several blocks. Is there anything you can do to make them stop?"

"I know you," one of the police officers said. "You're that guy who is all over the internet right now."

"That's right," the other cop interjected. "They were talking about you on the news."

"Right." I glanced over my shoulder at the women

growing nearer. Not only was I out of breath, but the tailored, one-of-a-kind suit that I was wearing for an important meeting I had was constricting, which meant I couldn't run as fast as I needed to run.

"Here's the thing," I said, slightly breathless. "Because of that internet mishap, I had random women knocking on the door of my hotel room all night. At first, I was pissed that the hotel had given out my room number, until I realized the women knocking all worked for the hotel. Then, my iPhone was constantly ringing off the hook to the point that I cut the damn thing off even though I need my phone to do business. I thought the hype would die down by the morning, but the moment I stepped into the lobby of my hotel, I was approached by the women you see running toward us right now and they have been chasing me ever since."

The police officers laughed, and the sound made me grind my teeth together. "Doesn't seem like a bad problem to have to me. Not sure what you want us to do."

My gaze bounced from one to the other. "Isn't it disturbing the peace by having a group of people running through intersections and cutting off the traffic flow?"

The skinny officer shrugged.

"What about giving them jaywalking tickets?"

"Then we'd have to give you one, too, according to what you've told us," the officer replied.

"Fine by me," I stated as calmly as possible. "Anything to end this morning from hell."

A squeal from a separate group of women to my left caught all our attention. "Not again," I whispered, noticing that look of recognition on a couple of the women's faces who'd just walked out of their office building.

The heftier police officer peered over his shoulder. "On

second thought, we don't see anything wrong. It looks to me as if this is one of the most exciting things to happen downtown in a while."

What the hell? "What about my well-being? I could be running for miles before they stop."

Instead of responding, each of the officers laughed. Concluding that neither of them were willing to help me, I took off running just as one officer asked if we could take a selfie together.

"I really worry about America right now," I huffed as I took a shortcut through an alley, almost running over a man taking out his garbage.

"Hey, watch yourself," the older gentleman yelled.

"Sorry," I called back. I glanced over my shoulder in time to see the herd of women knock him over, a few tumbling to the ground as they did so. A part of me thought this collision would make them stop, yet, the few who had fallen simply brushed off their knees, jumped right back up, and continued after me.

"This can't be real life." When I reached another busy road, I was slightly disoriented. It took a minute to realize that I'd walked into an area that was in the process of being set up for a food and wine festival occurring in a few days.

Glancing down at my cap toe Stacy Adams shoes, I cursed at the unfortunate events that had transpired in thirty-six hours. Now that I'd taken a detour, my cousins' lingerie boutique wasn't close anymore, but as luck would have it, I noticed that my brother's security firm was only a couple blocks away.

I need a distraction, I thought as I dodged in between two large semi-trucks that were being unloaded.

"Hey, man," I said to this young cat who couldn't have been more than twenty or twenty-one years old.

His eyes widened as if he recognized me, but to his credit, he didn't mention how. "Hello, sir."

"Hey." I pulled out a hundred-dollar bill. "I know you're working, but is there any way you could do me a solid and let me hide in this truck until the herd of women following me passes by?"

He looked skeptical at first, but he agreed. The feeling of relief that overwhelmed me was the best I'd felt all morning.

"What's your name?" I asked.

"Will," he replied.

I nodded in thanks. "Thank you, Will."

"No problem. I'll give you a holla when the coast is clear."

I almost wanted to hug him, but I knew it was just my adrenaline talking. Wasting no time, I passed him the hundred and climbed into the truck, hiding behind items that were waiting to be unloaded.

I loosened my tie, my heart beating out of my chest as I heard the voices of the women grow nearer. *This is a damn shame.* Who would have ever thought they'd see the day when Malakai Madden was hiding from a group of women?

I should have stayed my ass in New York. Business had brought me to Chicago, and since I had family in the area, it seemed like a great idea to stay for a little while and visit my siblings and cousins. Had I known that shit would hit the fan and I'd be dodging women left and right, I would have skipped this project and found myself a nice secluded bungalow in the Caribbean.

"Have you seen Malakai?"

I ducked deeper into the semi as I heard a woman ask Will where I was.

"Nah, I didn't see him," Will lied.

"Are you sure?" another woman asked. "He had to have come right past you."

"Maybe he's in the truck," a third woman chimed in.

Shit. In the midst of all the commotion, it dawned on me that I hadn't created an exit strategy when I'd gotten into this truck. There was only one way in and one way out, so if the women decided to search it, I couldn't escape.

"On second thought," Will began, "I think I saw him run that way."

I had no idea which way Will pointed, but I couldn't care less if it got them off my back.

"Let's go, ladies," one of them yelled. Soon, I heard the noise grow fainter as they left the semi.

I still felt as though I was on the brink of a heart attack as I waited for any indication that it was okay to leave. After a couple minutes, I assumed that Will had forgotten to give me the okay, so I proceeded to exit the truck.

It only took me a few seconds to assess the situation and realize that Will had still been looking out for me and my ass should have stayed in the back of the semi.

"There he is," a reporter yelled, turning from Will to me as I hopped out of the truck. "There's Malakai Madden."

The next thirty seconds seemed to happen in slow motion as I watched a group of reporters stumble over one another to get close to me.

"Mr. Madden, how does it feel to be the latest internet sensation?"

"Malakai, do you consider yourself a player or a one-woman man?"

"Malakai, you're a prominent artist and your clientele include a lot of celebrities and high-profiles politicians. But how do you think the release of this news will affect the churches and schools you do business with?"

I stood speechless as cameras flashed in my face and microphones were thrust in front of me. My mind could barely comprehend the questions being asked. I couldn't move as I thought about how much my life had been flipped upside down in thirty-six hours.

The lump in my throat made it hard for me to swallow as I contemplated the implications the internet madness would have on the personal goals I'd recently set for myself. Even worse, I couldn't begin to wrap my head around how this would affect my career.

I glanced over at Will who shrugged his shoulders in pity. I'd barely spoken with the dude, but today, he'd seen me at my worse. *This can't be happening.* I refused to think my life could change so much from a few tweets, but as I looked out over the crowd gathering to see what all of the fuss was about, I knew that was exactly what had happened.

Most men would love to have the media interested in interviewing them for such a spicy story. Most men would welcome a herd of women flocking behind him every second of the day. Most men would enjoy hearing women yell things that were better suited for bedroom banter, rather than in public.

"Malakai Madden, do you have anything to say?"

Too bad I wasn't most men.

ONCE UPON A BRIDESMAID

When four bridesmaids come together to support their best friend's wedding, they realize that most of the people they know have already tied the knot. Whether unlucky in love or single by choice, these besties make a pact to change their relationship status. The goal is simple... Each woman has one year to find Mr. Right and say 'I do'. Between passionate one-night-stands and best friend hookups, these bridesmaids are in for a wild ride. Are they in over their heads? Or will one impulsive wedding pact change their lives... forever.

Yours Forever excerpt on next page

Yours Forever by Sherelle Green (Book 1)

Beyond Forever by Elle Wright (Book 2)

Embracing Forever by Sheryl Lister (Book 3)

Hopelessly Forever by Angela Seals (Book 4)

The Pact

There are two things in life that a woman always needs to have in her possession: her sanity and her punani. Grandma Pearl's words echoed in Mackenzie Cannon's mind as she fidgeted in her cushioned wicker chair and ignored the conversation taking place between her best friends.

Grandma Pearl had always been one of Mac's favorite people. Not only had she been a classy woman with her large church hats and beautiful thick figure, but she'd also been the one to teach Mac the art of talking dirty without it sounding dirty.

Granted, there were times that Mac would rather say *pussy* instead of *punani*, but she kept it as classy as she could.

"I bet he tastes as good as he looks," Mac said aloud, taking in the delicious sight of the best man in a tux. "Can someone please get me a glass of water?"

When he turned to look her way, she didn't even try to

hide her thorough perusal of his body. Now that one of her best friends was married and dancing with her new husband on the dance floor, Mac could loosen her bridesmaid dress and focus on the tall cup of coffee who'd held her attention all weekend long.

"Seriously, Mac! Are you even listening to what I'm saying?"

Mac turned to face her best friend since childhood, Quinn Jacobs. They may be polar opposites, but Mac had a soft spot for Q. Despite their differences, they were extremely close. "I heard you, Q. I agree, Ava and Owen look happy. But in case you didn't notice, I'm trying my best focus on something a little more interesting than the newlyweds."

Mac, Quinn, Raven Emerson, and Ryleigh Fields had grown up in the small town of Rosewood Heights, South Carolina and had been friends since they were little girls. Although they each decided to pursue careers in other states, the women had returned to their hometown to celebrate the union of the fifth member of their pack—and the only friend still residing in Rosewood—Ava Prescott, to her husband, Owen Sullivan. The beautiful wedding had taken place in Rosewood Estates, a staple in the small lake town and perfect for a woman who valued tradition and community like Ava did.

"Why must you be so rude?" Raven asked, shaking her head. "You know how Q gets when she's talking about romance."

"Ha!" Mac said with a laugh. "Anyone within a thirty-mile radius can hear her squeal when she starts talking about love and shit."

"Girl, you can say that again," Ryleigh said, giving Mac a high-five. It was normal for Ryleigh and Mac to agree.

Both were headstrong and loved cozying up to a good-looking man every once and a while. At their high school dances, they'd often place bets on who could get the most numbers. Typically, they both took turns winning.

Quinn cleared her throat. "If everyone's done making fun of me, can we please continue the discussion?"

Mac turned her body in her chair so that she could face each of the women just as the waiter approached to take their drink order.

"I'll have another mojito," Mac said as she polished off her third glass in preparation for her fourth. When it came to getting through weddings, Mac had a firm drinking rule... More booze equaled more fun.

Conversation flowed between the friends as if it hadn't been a while since they'd last seen each other. Living in different states meant a lot of emails, calls, and text messages passed between them. Despite the different area codes, they made an effort to have a group conference call at least once a month to stay in touch.

The young waiter returned with their drinks and shot her what she assumed was his killer smile. Mac barely paid the youngin' any mind.

"I think we should toast," Quinn said, lifting her margarita high. "Here's to us all finding that special someone and saying 'I do' by this time next year."

Raven froze, her glass in mid-air. "Are you *crazy*?"

"Oh hell no," Ryleigh said at the same time, almost spilling her drink when she placed her glass on the table.

Mac was shaking her head in disagreement before Quinn even got out the last word. "The only thing I'm saying 'I do' to is one night with that tall, mouth-watering best man standing over there." She glanced over her shoulder in his direction.

Quinn placed her glass down and perked up in her chair. "Oh, come on you guys! We're twenty-nine years old! I don't want to be pushing a stroller when I'm fifty."

"If Janet Jackson can do it, so can we," Mac said with a smile.

"I'm being serious." Quinn scooted forward in her chair. "Think about it. Just about everybody we know has gotten married in the last three years, yet we're all still single. Wouldn't it be nice to have a warm, hard body to snuggle up to every night? To not have to worry about those awkward bar or club meetings? I mean, how hard could it be?" She lifted her glass again. "Come on! We can do this. Right here. Right now. Let's make a pact. Better yet, let's make this a best friend challenge."

Mac winced. *Damn, Q just said the magic words.* They were known to place a wager on anything and Mac *hated* to lose. Mac watched Raven slowly lift her glass to Quinn's. A quick glance at Ryleigh proved that she shared the same sentiment as Mac, but she slowly began to lift her glass as well.

"Oh shit," Mac huffed. "Are you seriously trying to make us all agree to be married before this time next year?"

Quinn smirked. "I thought the *Queen of Friends with Benefits* wasn't afraid of anything."

Mac rolled her eyes at the not-so-endearing nickname her friends had given her back when they were in high school. "I'm not afraid of anything."

"Then raise your glass, girlfriend," Quinn teased.

Mac hesitantly bit her bottom lip before finally raising her glass.

"To finding that special someone and saying 'I do' by this time next year," Quinn repeated when all four glasses were raised.

Mac felt like she was on auto-pilot as they clinked glasses before taking a sip of their drinks. *Screw it,* she thought as she downed her entire drink after a few more seconds. There weren't too many things that left Mac speechless, but agreeing to this pact was one for the books. *I definitely need a distraction now*, she thought as her eyes drifted back to the best man.

Mac stood from her chair. "Well, ladies, as fun as this is, I'll have to catch you in the morning for breakfast."

Quinn shook her head. "You won't find your husband by getting in the best man's pants."

Mac smoothed out her bridesmaid dress. "Sweetie, I'm sure my future husband, whomever he may be, will appreciate my sex drive. In the meantime, there are other men who will appreciate it just as much."

Was Mac ashamed that she enjoyed sex so much? Absolutely not. Would Mac ever apologize for having a frivolous fling? No way! She knew who she was and she didn't have to explain herself to anybody.

Quinn shook her head. "It's not always about sex, Mac."

"And marriage isn't always about love and romance." With a wink, Mac made her way across the room, leaving her friends to discuss how shocked they were that she'd agreed to the pact. They were probably assuming she would back out, but there was no way Mac was backing down from a best friend challenge. No way at all.

***

"Beware, my brother. You may have been tempted before, but temptation never looked like that."

Alexander Carter followed his brother's gaze, only to find the sexy bridesmaid that he'd been avoiding all weekend walking toward them. *Damn.* It was almost like she'd been plucked from every fantasy he'd ever had of the opposite sex. Her thick honey-brown curls were pulled to the side, cascading over her shoulders. Alex had always had a thing for big, natural curls and hers were no exception. His fingers itched to run through her hair.

If that wasn't enough to send his libido into overdrive, the woman had enough curves to keep a man occupied for decades. While some men always went after the skinny-model type, Alex preferred a woman with a little more meat on her bones. *And damned if she isn't stacked in all the right places.*

He cleared his throat before leaning against the bar and looking back at his younger brother, Shane. "Yeah, I'm in trouble."

"I told you, big bruh, you were in trouble the minute we went to Ava and Owen's luncheon a couple of days ago. When Owen asked us to be in the wedding last year, he warned you that Ava had some fine-ass friends."

"Yeah, but I didn't think he meant any of them were my type."

Shane laughed. "You know Owen has always been into talking in riddles and shit. He was trying to warn you without saying those exact words."

Alex shook his head. "I've been celibate for two years and haven't given into temptation. There's no way I'm giving in now."

Shane's voice lowered. "Listen, I know the face of a woman on a mission, so you have to ask yourself one question. Can you handle denying yourself a night with a sexy siren like her?"

"Yes, I can."

Shane could barely conceal his grin. "Then good luck, my brother." He glanced over Alex's shoulder. "You're gonna need it."

Shane had only been gone two seconds when she approached. "Hello, mind if I join you?"

Alex turned to face the stunning brown beauty he'd just been speaking about. *Tell her no. Send her on her way. You may have had the strength to avoid women before, but not a woman like her.*

"Sure, please do." Her thigh grazed his as she leaned next to him against the bar. Alex briefly shut his eyes. *Wrong move, my dude.*

"So, what is Alexander Carter's drink of choice?"

He took a sip of his once-forgotten drink. "Cognac on the rocks."

She squinted her eyes. "Smooth, strong, dark. At first it appears simple, but then you take one sip and experience the added element of charm and power." She looked him up and down. "I can see why you like it. It suits you."

Alex grinned slyly. "And what does Miss Mackenzie Cannon drink?"

"Today, mojitos were my drink of choice. But, usually, I'm a White Russian kind of woman."

Alex leaned slightly forward. "A White Russian... Sweet, yet robust. Creamy. The type of drink that sneaks up on you." He observed her a little closer. "And the coffee gives the drink a hint of the unexpected and plays with your taste buds."

When her eyes briefly danced with amusement, Alex noticed they were the color of sweet honey. He licked his lips and her eyes followed the movement.

"Very intuitive, Mr. Carter," Mac said as she stepped a little closer. "I'm not the type of woman to beat around the bush, so I must warn you that I came over here to try and seduce you."

Alex swallowed. "Well, I must say that you're doing a damn good job."

"Oh, I don't know about that, Mr. Carter." She pushed a few of her curls over her shoulder and placed one hand on her hip. "Although I came over here to do the seducing, you're seducing me in ways that you probably don't even realize."

Man, she needs to stop calling me Mr. Carter. Her voice was sultry and as smooth as velvet. Addressing him so formally was only making his pants tighter in the crotch area.

"Want to take a walk?" Mac asked.

If you leave the confides of this reception, you may not be able to control yourself. "Sure," he responded, ignoring the warning.

It was a beautiful September day in Rosewood Heights and Alex found the laid-back lake town extremely relaxing for a city boy like himself.

"I never thought I'd say this, but I miss this small town." Alex glanced at Mac just as she waved to a store owner across the street.

"I can understand why you miss it. I moved around so much as a kid that I don't really have roots anywhere. At least I didn't until I became an adult and settled down on the east coast."

"I know the feeling," Mac said with a laugh. "My family moved around a lot when I was younger, but for some reason, we always came back to Rosewood. And every time we returned, my girlfriends welcomed me back with open arms."

Alex smiled. He hadn't known Mac for more than forty-eight hours, but he'd pegged her as the type that didn't open up easily. The fact that she'd even told him that much surprised him.

They fell into easy conversation with an underline of flirtation in every word they said to one another. As much as Alex missed having sex, he missed the act of flirting even more. In his experience, flirting with a woman meant it would lead to other things. Things of the sexual nature. Things that wouldn't end well for a guy who'd made a vow of celibacy.

"I've done a lot of traveling, but this is still one of my favorite spots," Mac said as they approached a small garden with locks all along the fence. "We call this Love's Last Garden. It's been said that Rosewood Heights is the place where people come to relax and find love. Most of it is a myth, but this was the last garden that was built in the town and many townsfolk fell in love in this very place. Once you find love, you place a lock on the fence."

Alex looked around at the lush greenery and locks positioned about the fence. He couldn't quite place his finger on it, but he felt even more connected with Mac being in this garden. When he turned back to Mac, his eyes met hers. Watching him. Observing him. She bit her lip again in the same way he'd seen her do all day before her eyes dropped to his lips. *What is it with this woman?* He barely knew her, yet something about her drew him in. And without dwelling on his next move, he took two short strides toward her and pulled her to him.

He gave her a few seconds to protest, but when she looked up at him expectantly, he brought his lips down to hers. Alex had meant for it to be a simple kiss, but he should have known that Mac would awaken a desire deep within him, especially after the tension between them all weekend.

She slowly opened her mouth and he took the invitation to add his tongue to the foreplay.

Kissing Mac wasn't what he'd expected. It was so much more. He may be celibate, but he'd had his fair share of kisses. With Mac, she kissed with her entire body, nipping and suckling in a way that was mentally breaking down the walls he usually had up. When her moan drifted to his ears, Alex pulled her even closer, tilting her head for better access. His hands eventually found their way to her ass, cupping her through the material of her dress. Although the sun had set, they kissed in a way that made Alex forget that they were standing in a public garden.

At her next moan, Alex stepped back. *Man, you need to get a grip.* Even with the space between them, he could still feel her heat. If she kissed like that, he could only imagine how she'd be in bed.

They stood there for a couple of minutes, neither saying anything as they took in their fill of one another. Being the CEO of an environmental engineer firm, Alex knew a thing or two about self-control to reach the ultimate goal. He was one of the most controlled people he knew. However, as he got lost in Mac's honey gaze, he couldn't remember the reasons why he'd decided to be celibate in the first place. *Surely there were a list of reasons, right?*

Mac stepped back to him and ran her fingers over his loosened navy blue tie. "Your room or mine?"

This was it. This was the situation he'd been trying to avoid since he'd laid eyes on Mackenzie Carter. The old Alex wouldn't have hesitated to drag Mac to his hotel room and explore her delicious body. However, the new and improved Alex didn't think it was such a good idea. His right and wrong consciousness battled with one another, each arguing their point of view, trying to convince him to take their side. *This should be an easy decision. Say no, remain celibate, and send Mac on her merry way.*

"What will it be, Mr. Carter?" She brought her plump lips to his ear. "Do you want to share a night of unrestrained bliss with yours truly?" She tugged his earlobe between her teeth before soothing the bite with a kiss.

What. The. Fuck. If there was a book on seduction, Mac must have invented it. When she boldly ran her hips over his mid-section, he lost all train of thought. His eyes landed on hers and held her gaze.

"Mine," he said in a firm voice. "It's time that I show you what calling me 'Mr. Carter' does to me."

He didn't even give her a chance to respond as he tugged her through the garden and in the direction of Rosewood Inn.

HIGH CLASS SOCIETY SERIES

In a society of trust fund babies, millionaires and upper-class peers, four women seeking a prestigious ivy league education were thrust into a privileged world of wealth and aristocrats. Overwhelmed by the segregation they witnessed in the university that forced students to date within their own social class, they decide to create a world not based on society's rules. An organization in which the everyday woman not given the chance to date a person of caliber can overcome the barriers placed before her and date whomever she pleases.

There are no limits to finding love and they simply supply women the tools and encouragement to go after the person they want in hopes that it results in a successful relationship. Hence, after graduating from college in 2006, High Class Society Incorporated was established. Now, years later, although all four founding women have established successful careers, the secret organization is in full effect. But like every secret society, the biggest obstacle is keeping it a secret.

Blue Sapphire Temptation by Sherelle Green (Book 1)

Her Sweetest Seduction by Angela Seals (Book 2)

Sealed with a Kiss by Angela Seals (Book 3)

Passionate Persuasion by Sherelle Green (Book 4)

MEET LOGAN "LO" AND TRISTAN

Logan "Lo" Sapphire has never backed down from a challenge, so she's convinced that she can persuade the stern and unyielding self-made millionaire to keep High Class Society a secret after he bursts into her office demanding to know his sister's whereabouts. The last thing Lo wants to do is go on a wild goose chase with a walking sex ad to find his sister, but maybe, just maybe, finding her will coax him into signing a confidentiality agreement.

Tristan Derrington has a reputation for doing what he wants, when he wants. Usually nothing will stop Tristan from pursuing a gorgeous beauty like Logan, but even temptation in four-inch heels won't stand in the way of him finding his sister and exposing HCS. He may think he has a solid plan to avoid their obvious attraction, but even the best laid plans can fail. The more time they spend together, the harder it is to deny their explosive chemistry. Especially when they realize how delicious giving into temptation can be.

Prologue

January 2006
Yale University

"That's it! I'm done wasting my time on these snobbish boys who think more with their wallets than their minds."

Logan Sapphire looked up from her notebook as her friend Harper Rose entered their apartment.

"I'm guessing the date didn't go well."

Harper huffed. "Let's try terrible. Horrible. Possibly the worst date of my entire life."

"Maybe you're forgetting about that frat guy you went out with two months ago," said their other roommate, Peyton Davis, as she entered the living room and took a seat on the chair opposite Logan. "If I remember correctly, he rushed your date because he had to take out that freshman and he actually had the nerve to tell you that."

"Oh right," Harper said as she kicked off her heels and plopped on the couch. "Yeah, he was pretty bad."

All three ladies glanced at the door as their fourth roommate, Savannah Westbrook, entered the apartment lugging a book bag, tote bag, and laptop bag that she immediately dropped at the entrance. Logan never did understand why Savannah always carried around so much stuff, but that was Savannah. She was always researching, studying, or doing something that required her to take her notes, books and laptop everywhere.

"What did I miss?" Savannah asked as she sat on the couch next to Harper.

Harper sighed. "Just me ranting about my sorry excuse for a date with that arrogant jerk I went out with tonight."

"Wait, isn't he that fine guy from your photo journalism class that you were dying to go out with? I thought he seemed different than the others."

"They're all the same," Harper replied. "Not only did he spend most the night talking about himself, his money, and his dad's company that he was going to be working at right after graduation. But then he had the nerve to slip me a key card for the hotel room he'd booked for the night."

"What did you tell him?" Logan asked. Harper was the insightful one in the group so there was no doubt in her mind that Harper tried to explain to him exactly why he was an arrogant jerk instead of just cursing him out. She was the one who didn't just take things from surface value, but instead, she always took a deeper look.

"He told me that most women would jump at the opportunity to have sex with him on a first date. So I told him all the reasons why he would never get into my panties."

"The nerve of these guys. See, this is the only reason why I regret not going to a regular university. There are some real pretentious assholes here," Peyton chimed in.

"And even if you're lucky enough to find a *trust fund* guy here who is actually decent, you run into issues with his friends and family accepting you," Logan added. Although she was currently engaged to one of those *privileged* men and had been dating him for most of college, she couldn't help that feeling in the pit of her stomach. That feeling that warned her she was making the wrong decision by marrying him after college and joining a family that didn't accept her or think she was worthy enough to carry their last name. She didn't date him for his money, but his family didn't see it that way.

"We aren't the only women with these issues," Savannah stated. "Just last week, I was talking to perky Paula, who couldn't stop crying in class after her boyfriend of three years broke up with her."

Logan shook her head in disbelief. "They were so in love. Please tell me it's not because her family had to file for bankruptcy."

"You guessed it," Savannah confirmed. "Apparently, being with someone who no longer has money isn't a good look. Three years down the drain."

"See, I worked my ass off to get here," Harper said. "Being from a low or middle-class family shouldn't make me less worthy of love than someone born from money. Isn't love about finding your soul mate and the person you want to spend the rest of your life with? Wouldn't you rather have a hardworking woman by your side, money or no money?"

Peyton leaned over and slapped hands with Harper. "Agreed. And the opening line on a date shouldn't be how much my family makes or how dating me can improve or decrease their social status."

Logan glanced around at her friends as they began

sharing stories that they'd heard around campus from women who had fallen for a guy only to realize that because of social status, they couldn't be together. Logan and her roommates were all from hard-working families and each had worked hard to get accepted into Yale on scholarship and follow their dreams. They didn't major in the same discipline, but they'd instantly connected during freshman orientation week and had been close all through college. Even though it was their last semester, she was certain they would remain friends after graduation and already, the four-some was planning on moving to New York together.

"You know what's crazy," Logan said finally closing her notebook and placing it on the coffee table. "We each gained so much by attending Yale, but I think you all agree that we've never faced this much adversity when it came to dating and by the sound of it, there are so many ladies on campus that are in the same boat as we are. And not just here at Yale, I'm sure this is an issue outside of school as well."

Harper nodded her head in agreement. "I think you're right. My cousin went through a similar issue with liking a man she met at a business conference. She said he was really interested in her as well, but after spending the first two conference days together, he was pulled in several different directions by other women."

"So he just stopped talking to her?" Logan asked.

"Sort of. See, at her company she's an executive assistant, which is a great position and she really loves it. She accompanied the president of her company on the trip. But the women approaching the man she was interested in were all VP's, Presidents of other companies or women who were part of a family that sponsored the conference. Since his organization was planning the conference, his job as

CEO of the event was to wine and dine all clients to try and get new business."

Logan began seeing the bigger picture. "So basically, he was interested, but because of obligations to talk to the other women, he couldn't spend as much time with her."

"That's right. But I told her that I felt like she should have just continued to talk to him like she had been. She wasn't invited to every event at the conference, but she was invited to enough where she could have pushed past those women and made an effort."

"Easier said than done," Savannah said. "It's one thing to know a man is interested. It's another issue entirely to have the confidence not to care about what the other people in attendance think and convince yourself that you're bold enough to talk to him."

"I agree with Savannah," Peyton said. "Sometimes it's about self-confidence and the idea that you aren't any different than the other women vying for his attention. All men who have money or were born from money don't only want to date women from influential families. We run into that a lot here at Yale, but I guess we have to keep in mind that we are dealing with boys trying to be men. Not men who already know what they want and don't care about what others think."

"Those men are out there," Logan added with a sly smile. "We just have to find them."

Harper squinted her eyes at Logan. "Lo, I know that look. What are you thinking?"

"Do you guys remember last year when we were sitting around drinking wine after celebrating Savannah's twenty-first birthday?"

They all nodded their head in agreement. "Do you remember what we discussed that night?"

Savannah scrunched her head in thought. "Was that the time we stayed up all night discussing what it would be like in a world that didn't have typical dating rules that you had to follow? I think we talked about how it would be if we could date good men and not worry about whether or not money, family names, or social standing would be an issue."

"Exactly," Logan said snapping her fingers. "Peyton, you said you would love it if we could start our own organization. Then Harper, you started talking about how great it would be if it were a secret organization that no one knew about. Then Savannah, you and I started talking about the way the organization could work and how great it would be if we also encouraged women to pursue love and help build their self-esteem. Especially if their self-esteem was damaged as a result of a bad relationship."

"Um, so what exactly are you getting at?" Peyton asked inquisitively. "Because it sounds a lot like you're trying to say we should turn the ideas we had that day into reality."

Logan smiled and clasped her hands together as she looked at each roommate.

"Oh no," Savannah said shaking her head. "That's precisely what you're trying to say isn't it?"

"Come on guys, you all have to admit that our ideas that night were pretty amazing."

"I'm pretty sure I was tipsy," Harper mentioned.

"No you weren't. We had just started drinking our first glass when we talked about this." Logan got up from her chair and began pacing the room as her brain began working overtime.

"Hear me out ladies. Peyton, you have amazing business sense and there is no doubt in my mind that you have what it takes to handle the ins and outs of a secret organization. Savannah, you're amazing at researching and like we discussed last year, it would be great if we could develop profiles of eligible bachelors, but they have to be the right type of men. Harper, you're a wiz with marketing and social media. Private or not, we will definitely need that. And of course, since I'm majoring in human resources, I could handle meeting and conversing with the members."

She turned and was greeted with blank stares from all three women, so she continued talking. "I know we would have to work out a lot of kinks and really solidify our business plan, but there is no doubt in my mind that we were on to something great the night of Savannah's birthday and I'm sure, if we put our minds to it, we could create something amazing. A secret society unlike any other."

When their faces still displayed blank stares, she'd thought maybe she was talking too fast and they hadn't heard her. She was relieved when Harper's mouth curled to the side in a smile.

"I can't believe I'm saying this, but I honestly loved the idea when we first came up with it last year, and I love it even more now that we're graduating. Off hand, I can already think about several women who would be more than happy to join."

"So, we're really going to do this?" Savannah said with a smile. "We are actually going to start our own secret society?"

"Not just any society," Peyton said as she stood to join Logan. "Didn't we create some guidelines for the organization that night?"

"I think I have all our notes from that," Logan said as she ran to her room to grab her laptop and returned to the living room. She kneeled down at the coffee table, opened up a word document, and was joined by Harper, Savannah and Peyton who kneeled down around her laptop as well.

"Here it is. All our notes from that night."

Savannah pointed to sentence. "Oh wow, it says here that we thought members should have to take a rigorous personal, professional and spiritual assessment when they join before they are placed in a position to meet quality matches."

Harper pointed to another sentence. "And here it says that we will build well-researched profiles on eligible bachelors and give women the tools and encouragement to go after the man of their dreams."

"So we decided that this wouldn't be a match making service right?" Peyton asked the group. "We would place women in a position to meet a man they are interested in, but we aren't playing matchmaker and setting them up on a date."

"That seems accurate to what we discussed," Logan answered. "But of course, we'll have to get all those details nailed down before inviting members."

"Didn't we come up with a name too?" Peyton asked searching the notes on the page.

Logan scrolled down until she landed on the page she was searching for.

"High Class Society Incorporated," she said aloud to the group. "That was the name we created last year."

Harper clasped her hands together. "Oh I remember now! I still love that name."

"Me too," Savannah and Peyton said in unison.

Logan pointed her finger to the words on the screen written underneath the name of the organization and read them aloud. "There are no limits to finding love, no rulebook to discover your soul mate, and no concrete path to follow in order to reach your destiny. In High Class Society, we make that journey a little easier. High Class Society ... where elite and ordinary meet."

She looked up at each of the ladies, each with a knowing gleam in their eyes. This year didn't just mark their graduation and start of their careers. It also marked the beginning of a new chapter for the four of them. A chapter that was sure to be filled with pages and pages of new self-discoveries

Chapter 1

9 years later...

"You have *one* minute to tell me where the hell my sister is, or I'll have no choice but to call the authorities and expose this disgraceful ass company."

The deep timbre in the man's voice bounced off the burgundy walls of the Manhattan office and teased Logan's ears. Her big, doe-eyes stared at the sexy intruder with the rich, mocha skin tone as she tried her best not to drop her mouth open in admiration. She knew who he was. Her company had done their research on him when Logan had first met his sister. They were actually in the process of gathering further information on him to build a more solid profile and add him to their list of exceptional men. However, the pictures definitely didn't do this former Canadian turned New Yorker justice.

In the profile she'd received from her partner and friend, Savannah Westbrook, the Director of Research and Development for High Class Society, she could tell he was a walking sex ad. Even after recognizing his clearly masculine sex appeal, she couldn't have prepared herself for the onslaught of pleasure she'd feel coming face-to-face with temptation.

Her eyes wandered up and down the length of his body that was encased in a deep-blue Tom Ford suit, complementing leather shoes, and a classic navy-blue watch with gold trimmings. Licking her lips as she admired his six-foot frame, she tried not to imagine how enticing he'd look without a stitch of clothing on. Usually Logan was attracted to men with curly hair and a caramel complexion, but the man standing before her didn't have either of those qualities ... and damned if she even cared. Within a few seconds, she'd dismissed every physical characteristic she'd ever believed she wanted in a man. *Delicious,* she thought after taking note of his short fade and chiseled jawline, his neatly groomed features mirroring that of a Tyson Beckford look-alike rather than Shemar Moore.

"I'm so sorry, Lo," said her assistant, Nina, a grad student at Columbia University, as she came rushing in to the office behind the unwelcomed guest. "I'm not sure how he even got clearance into the building or how he found your office."

"It wasn't hard to find your office with so few people here and a distracted security guard," he explained, his eyes never straying from Logan. His piercing gaze was so intense that Logan was glad she was sitting at her desk or she would have surely faltered. "And you should really lock up the bathroom window in the basement. I climbed right in."

She tilted her head to the side, unable to believe that a man of his status would climb through a window to get into their office.

"It's okay, Nina," she reassured, refusing to break their stare-down. "I'll listen to what Mr. Derrington has to say."

Nina hesitantly exited the office and left the door cracked, instead of closing it all the way like she normally would when Logan had a meeting.

"Ms. Sapphire, I take it that you already know who I am," he stated with a slight curl of his lips. *Don't do that,* she thought when he walked a little closer to her desk. His imposing stance was already sending her body into a frenzy. She couldn't stay seated and let him have the upper hand.

"It appears you already know who I am as well, Mr. Derrington." Rising from her seat, she noted the appreciative glance he shot in her direction. She smoothed out her designer skirt and blouse before sitting on the edge of her desk. His eyes ventured to her creamy, maple thighs before making their way to the swell of her breasts.

Logan's breath caught as she watched him observe her. She was hardly showing any cleavage and her clothes were concealing all of her assets. Yet the way he was staring at her, made her feel as if she wasn't wearing anything at all. The air around them was thick with awareness, and the silence almost caused her to fidget under his stare.

"I've been away on business and came back early because I hadn't heard from my younger sister. So I went to her condo, and imagine my surprise when I surfed her laptop, trying to find some information about her whereabouts, and saw several screen shots saved in a folder on her desktop entitled High Class Society Incorporated."

Logan winced at his statement, silently cursing his discovery. HCS prided themselves on being paperless, a key to keeping the organization a secret. Unfortunately, no matter how good their small IT team was, some things were hard to avoid ... like members taking screen shots containing information that couldn't get out to the public.

"Ms. Sapphire, after I got over the shock of an organization like yours existing, I researched the duties of the founders listed on one of the screen shots and realized that you may be the only person to know where my sister is.

According to what I read, all women are supposed to check in daily with you if they're away with a prospect, correct?"

"That is true," Logan responded. "May I remind you that the contents on those screen shots are private, and my organization did not approve for your sister to go off on her own before finishing part two of her orientation session, including our policy on safety."

"So she *is* with a man," he said more to himself than her. His jaw twitched and he placed both hands in his pockets, frustration radiating from his body. "May I remind *you* that as long as my sister is missing, everything is my business. She wouldn't have gotten this idea to run off with God knows who if your company didn't exist."

"We help women find the person of their dreams, Mr. Derrington. We have rules, which she didn't follow. We aren't babysitters."

"I assume I don't need to reinforce that I'll sue you for all your worth if you don't tell me what I need to know, Ms. Sapphire ... if that's even your real last name."

"It is," she stated firmly. "I have nothing to hide, and although this is against my better judgment, I will tell you who she's with," she continued, purposely leaving out the fact that she didn't know where Sophia was. She did have something to hide, but she needed to bluff to buy her and her partners some time before he went to the authorities.

"So," he said, removing both hands from his pockets and waving them for her to explain, "who is my sister with?"

Logan sighed, still not okay with sharing the information, but she knew he wasn't leaving without an answer. "She's with social media prodigy, Justice Covington."

She watched all of the color drain from his face while both hands curled into fists. His breathing grew heavier and he slowly rolled his neck ... purposeful ... measured. Logan found her own breathing growing labored as she sat and watched a range of emotions cross his face.

"Then we definitely have a problem," he stated as he released his fists and leaned in closer to her, "because Justice Covington met my sister when she was eighteen and they tried to get married two years ago. If we don't find them, he may finally get his wish ... *if* they haven't tied the knot already."

***

30 minutes earlier ...

"Where are you?" Logan Sapphire asked aloud as she scrolled through the online files she had for one of the newest clients to High Class Society, Sophia Derrington. Her cherry-colored office desk—that was usually extremely organized—was covered in an array of paperwork and maps she'd printed to try and piece together where Sophia might be. In all of her eight years of being Director of HR and Recruiting, she'd never lost contact with a client for this long.

"What the hell am I going to do?" she huffed aloud, standing up and running her French tipped fingernails through her thick and wavy copper-colored hair. She paced back and forth in her office, glad that her partners had all retired for the night. Only Logan and her assistant remained, and she was extremely thankful that Nina had decided to help her search for Sophia, despite the fact that Nina felt partially responsible.

Sophia hadn't been born from wealth, but thirty-four-year-old Tristan Derrington, Sophia's older brother, was a self-made millionaire and one of the most sought after custom watch designers in the country. He created top-notch designs for numerous celebrities, singers, hip-hop artists, and political figures. High Class Society had certain rules, and one of them was to ensure that the only women allowed in the society were women who weren't born from money or from highly privileged families. They were all successful professionals and entrepreneurs, or self-made millionaires. Of course, sometimes rules were meant to be broken, and in some instances, they made an exception and allowed a woman to join who was born from money or a well-known family. Those situations were handled on a case-by-case basis.

Even though it seemed unfair, Logan and her partners had strict rules that they had to adhere to in order to ensure that High Class Society was successful and effective. They didn't just let any woman into the organization. Each woman went through a psychological, spiritual, and professional screening to ensure that they were truly looking for love and not a gold-digging groupie. Their clientele consisted of women of different nationalities, ethnic backgrounds, and occupations, and they were proud of the successful relationships that had developed from their company.

Logan stopped pacing and abruptly sat down in her desk chair, accidently knocking over a cup of black coffee as she did so. "Shit," she cursed, quickly grabbing some nearby napkins and dabbing up the coffee.

"Are you okay?" Nina yelled from outside of her office.

"I'm fine," she yelled back after she'd wiped up most of the coffee and waved the wet stained paperwork in the air to dry it quicker.

Focus, Logan! she thought to herself as she leaned back

in her chair and clasped her hands in her lap. *Are there any clues in the last conversation you had with Sophia?*

Ever since she'd first met Sophia months ago, the twenty-four year old had wormed her way into Logan's heart after divulging the story about how she'd lost the only man she had ever loved and was ready to see what else was out there. She'd claimed she needed High Class Society, and Logan had chosen to ignore the signs that something more was going on. Now that she had no idea where Sophia had run off to, she had time to reflect on the fact that Sophia had only shown interest in one man ... Justice Covington. HCS always listed possible matches in each woman's personal online folder and Sophia had included other men in her profile as "persons of interest," but any time Logan had spoken with Sophia, the young lady had only asked her about Justice, the thirty-two-year-old brain behind an up and coming social media network.

Closing her eyes, she thought back to the information she'd given Sophia about Justice attending a Broadway play at the Ethel Barrymore Theatre here in New York. She had warned Sophia to focus on men closer to her own age, but she'd been determined to meet Justice. That was the last day they'd spoken almost two weeks ago. Since then, she'd only received one text from Sophia saying that she was okay and was following her heart. All of their HCS ladies knew they had to check in daily if they were going away with a man, so she was worried and pissed that Sophia was jeopardizing the company and going rogue.

"What am I missing?" she wondered aloud before going on her computer to look at the personal file they had on Justice Covington again. There was a reason Sophia was interested in Justice, and why Savannah hadn't been able to track Justice's whereabouts lately in regards to his relation-ship status. Something wasn't adding up.

"Sir, you can't go in there," she heard Nina yell right before a man walked into her office, literally taking her breath away. *Tristan Derrington ... in the flesh.* God, he was sexy. Although she wished she could relish in his presence, the fact that he was standing in her office meant that HCS was in more trouble than she knew.

ABOUT THE AUTHOR

Sherelle Green is a Chicago native with a dynamic imagination and a passion for reading and writing. Ever since she was a little girl, Sherelle has enjoyed story-telling. Upon receiving her BA in English, she decided to test her skills by composing a fifty-page romance. The short, but sweet, story only teased her creative mind, but it gave her the motivation she needed to follow her dream of becoming a published author.

Sherelle loves connecting with readers and other literary enthusiasts, and she is a member of RWA and NINC. She's an award winning author and two-time RT Book Reviews nominee. Sherelle enjoys composing novels that are emotionally driven and convey real relationships and real-life issues that touch on subjects that may pull at your heartstrings. Nothing satisfies her more than writing stories filled with compelling love affairs, multifaceted characters, and intriguing relationships.

For more information:
www.sherellegreen.com
authorsherellegreen.com

Made in the USA
Middletown, DE
27 July 2020

13647503R00151